The Story of
ADAMSVILLE

Agnes Riedmann

Wadsworth Publishing Company
Belmont, California
A division of Wadsworth, Inc.

Sociology Editor: Curt Peoples
Editorial/Production Services: Phoenix Publishing Services
Cover Design: Alan May

ISBN 0-534-00823-2

© 1980 by Wadsworth, Inc.

© 1977 by Wadsworth Publishing Company, Inc. All rights reserved. No part of this book may be reproduced, stored in a retrieval system, or transcribed, in any form or by any means, electronic, mechanical, photocopying, recording, or otherwise, without the prior written permission of the publisher, Wadsworth Publishing Company, Belmont, California 94002, a division of Wadsworth, Inc.

Printed in the United States of America

6   7   8   9   10—90   89   88   87   86

Library of Congress Cataloging in Publication Data

Riedmann, Agnes Czerwinski.
    The story of Adamsville.

    I. Title.
PZ4.R549St   [PS3568.I363]   813'.5'4   79-25624
ISBN 0-534-00823-2

Contents

Introduction	*v*
Prologue	*2*
Episode 2	*8*
Episode 3	*14*
Episode 4	*20*
Episode 5	*28*
Episode 6	*36*
Episode 7	*42*
Episode 8	*48*
Episode 9	*54*
Episode 10	*62*
Episode 11	*68*
Episode 12	*74*
Episode 13	*80*
Episode 14	*88*
Episode 15	*94*
Episode 16	*100*
Episode 17	*104*
Episode 18	*108*
Episode 19	*112*

DEDICATED TO
Edmund M. Czerwinski, my father,
and
Ann Langley Czerwinski, my mother

ACKNOWLEDGMENTS
go to Bill Riedmann for his love, support, and friendship; and to Christine Langley, Lorraine Duggin, Sheryl Fullerton, and Stephen Rutter for their creative ideas and critical help.

Introduction

The Story of Adamsville is science fiction. I wrote it to dramatize basic sociological concepts. Gabriel Knapp, the main character, is a human mutant living in the early twenty-first century. He is a citizen of Adamsville, a growing colony of mutants located in a desert in the southwestern United States. The mutants, called "greens," look normal until they are about twenty-five years old, when the skin can be expected to turn green because of the chlorophyll it contains. As greens near the end of the normal period, they often "pass," meaning that they choose to live or work temporarily outside Adamsville in the larger society.

Gabe, a "passing" green, attempts to live in two cultures at once only to find himself a victim of divided loyalties. Raised in Adamsville, he has attended college on the outside and is now successfully employed among nonmutants as an insurance executive. Still appearing normal, he falls in love with Monica Roanoke, a nonmutant attorney who practices in Chicago. All that happens to Gabe and the choices he makes combine to illustrate the power—and the relativity—of cultural beliefs, values, and norms.

The term *culture,* as used by sociologists, refers to those symbols, beliefs, and values that members of a given group or society hold in common. Human beings, as far as we know, do not inherit culture genetically (as they do, for example, the color of their eyes, the shape of their bodies, and the complexion of their skin). Rather, they fashion cultural environments through social interaction. They agree, whether consciously or unconsciously, that certain beliefs are true, that certain behaviors are good, and that certain values are right while others (beliefs, behaviors, values) are false, bad, or wrong. By means of this continuous process, cultural reality is socially constructed.

How individuals and groups participate in constructing social reality is a major theme of *The Story of Adamsville.* In Episode 18, for example, we see how a mass medium (and by extension, all mass media)—in this case, newspapers—can influence public opinion and thereby help to shape cultural agreements. Even the "reality" of physical illness can be socially constructed as in the case of Ann Sullivan (Episode 16), whose chronic depression and general lethargy is caused by the belief in Adamsville that she is "genetically impoverished."

Because groups create their own peculiar realities, the variety of human cultures is great. The term *cultural relativity* is used to describe the belief that each culture is legitimate in its own right. In the contrast of green culture to that of the larger society, cultural relativity emerges as a major theme.

Culture is a power of inestimable force, because once it is created and established, it becomes *reified:* All the beliefs, values, and norms constituting it come to be taken as hard and fast truth. The mutants, for example, agreed to call their settlement *Adamsville*. Once this agreement was made, it became a truth as well as a value. The mutants felt it was *wrong* to call the colony by any other name.

Striking evidence of the power of cultural agreements to shape behavior is embodied in the concept of the self-fulfilling prophecy. A *self-fulfilling prophecy* is one in which a predicted event comes to pass because the prediction itself causes it to. Several self-fulfilling prophecies are worked out in this story. In Episode 11, for example, Gabriel loses his job outside Adamsville because, as his boss explains, "We know that greens make a practice of returning to Green Colony at just about the time they have become most valuable to their employers." This generalization, when applied to Gabe, becomes a prediction and helps cause what it predicts—Gabe's return to Adamsville. Self-fulfilling prophecies not only indicate the power of culture to influence, and sometimes determine, behavior but also reinforce the agreement that reality is indeed socially constructed.

The way in which a social reality gets created is described in the Prologue as the evolutionary scientists, dealing with an undefined—and therefore confusing—situation offer opposing theories about the nature, origin, and culture of the mutants. In his urgent meeting with his secretary of the interior, the president of the United States is agitated and indecisive. Because the newly discovered creatures have not yet been *socially defined,* he is unable to develop a national policy concerning greens. He says of the mutants, "We can't even be sure they have civil rights. We haven't yet decided whether the things are *human.*"

The definition of social reality—and the subsequent creation of cultural beliefs and values—invariably results in power struggles among political and religious factions within a particular society. Those who succeed in gaining power are better able, although not necessarily better qualified, to define reality as they choose. In Episode 6, for instance, the Association for the Prevention of Infant Kidnappings and the Society for the Protection of the Human Race serve as examples of *voluntary associations* whose members share common views. By pooling their collective power, they hope to exert significant political influence over the eventual definition of greens.

Factions also emerge within Adamsville. The dispute in Episode

INTRODUCTION   vii

15 over who should be sent to the third conference on human mutations exemplifies the way in which intragroup conflict can weaken group solidarity. *Class conflict* and struggle for power are also illustrated in the political infights between bright greens and dull, or "milkwhite," greens.

Whether or not greens are human, the fact remains that they have created a culture. Depicting many cultural symbols, beliefs, values, and norms in Adamsville, Episode 4 shows how people in any culture tend to justify (or reinforce) their values by their beliefs and their norms (socially expected behaviors) by their values. The mutants believe, for example, that green chromosomes are always dominant and that any mutant raised outside Adamsville will die. Together, these beliefs support the value that it is "good" to rescue mutant babies born outside Adamsville. That value, in turn, sanctions—and thereby dictates—the norm of kidnapping. Similarly, the value statement, "Eating is a weakness," justifies the normative restriction against going to restaurants. We can view the greens as a *subculture* within American society, sharing some agreements with the larger society, clearly departing from others, and adapting still others.

Subcultural agreements, like those of the dominant or larger culture, are not only created but also learned. The central theme in Episode 5 centers around Gabriel's personal dilemmas in attempting to socialize himself into two cultures at the same time. *Socialization* is the process by which a society transmits its cultural beliefs, values, and norms to new generations. *Internalization,* on the other hand, is the process whereby individuals learn, or "take in," their culture in order to develop identities. It becomes apparent in Episode 5 that despite his adult participation in the nongreen world, Gabe's identity—his sense of self—is that of a green. He has internalized the beliefs, values, and norms of greens to the point where he feels homesick for Adamsville and experiences the Fourth of July as a meaningless holiday. He longs instead to celebrate Adam's birthday. More important, perhaps, he continues to feel obligated to be a rescuer—a role learned through childhood games. The episode also relates examples of family, peer, school, and adult socialization.

A secondary theme that has emerged by Episode 5 is the *role conflict* that Gabriel experiences as a result of his participation in two different cultures. Role conflict pertains to the problems of ambivalence that arise when an individual occupies two statuses that carry incompatible role expectations. As Monica's supposedly nongreen lover, Gabe is expected to be hungry and enthusiastic at the July Fourth picnic. As a green, however, he has learned to minimize the importance of eating (and its joys), perceiving it as he was taught, as a sign of weakness.

Gabe's role conflict is illustrated even more dramatically in Episode 7. What has been a friendship between two people, Gabe and Monica, is drastically altered once the "truth" about Gabriel's identity is known and the situation is subjected to the couple's social definitions of reality. Their relationship is threatened by two conflicting cultural versions of reality. From Gabe's point of view, his act of returning an infant to Adamsville was a "rescue"; to Monica, it was a "kidnapping," a serious moral wrong and a poignant example of *deviant behavior*. As Gabe sees it, he is rescuing a child from "birthers" (nongreens) who don't love their children. According to Monica, the infant was taken from his "real" parents, who are now grief stricken. Here the reader might speculate about the nature of parental grief over the loss of a child: Is it something that is culturally learned, or is parental grief a "natural" and universal experience among all human beings? Whichever is true, Episode 7 points out how personal experience is filtered through a screen of firmly established, or *institutionalized*, cultural agreements. Institutionalized beliefs, values, and norms can become so totally reified that people lose sight of their existence as social agreements.

Episodes 8, 9, and 10 focus on the way in which basic social institutions are organized in Adamsville. In Episode 8, we see that the institutional arrangements for *family* life and child rearing are quite different from those of our society. Adults enter into nurturing contracts for the purpose of raising children. Nurturing parents are not expected to be the biological parents; they may be of the same or opposite sex; and they may number more than two people. In Adamsville, since the social role of parent is unrelated to romantic love, greens take it for granted that the contract to nurture until the child's eighteenth birthday will not be broken. Divorce, obviously, is not a problem. An interesting question for the reader to pose at this point is whether a cultural arrangement such as this would be feasible in our society.

By Episode 9, Gabe's distress over his many sins—using supplement, failing to turn fully green, failing to return to Adamsville when he should have, smoking tobacco—illustrates the potential impact of *religion* on individuals. Moreover, it becomes evident that religious beliefs can justify or legitimate the organization of a society. The religious belief, for example, that greens fail to brighten in color because of spiritual disloyalty justifies the value and practice of giving brighter greens a higher status in the colony.

The descriptions of rituals in Adamsville—the funeral rites and maturation rites, for example—demonstrate how religious rituals function as active and collective expressions of religious dogma. The beliefs are not only stated in the celebration, they are acted out as well.

In Adamsville, the institution of religion is *integrated* with both family and *education*. Children learn Adam's teachings about God's plan from their parents and their teachers. Gabriel, however, upon attending a "foreign" university, found scientific evidence that challenged his faith. Larry Jones, the self-appointed and charismatic religious leader in Adamsville, aims to counter these religious aberrations by further integrating his colony's religion with education. To combat potential heresy, he would establish a university within Adamsville, founding it on the tenets of his fundamentalist philosophy.

Integration of the *economic* and *political* institutions is illustrated in Episode 10. Several of the pressure groups demonstrating outside the National Conference on Human Mutations take political positions that are closely allied with their economic self-interests. Larry Jones' political power seems to derive as much from his demonstrated economic success as from his dazzling skin color. Political and economic institutions are in turn integrated with religion. Government in the colony illustrates what Max Weber called the *traditional type of authority* and operates through a theocratic merging of the sacred and the secular.

In spite of the fact that greens have created a complex and integrated culture, many nongreens persist in viewing them as subhuman. Within the framework of the larger society, a *caste system* seems imminent. In Episode 11 the privileges and civil rights that have been granted Gabe as a matter of course on the outside are now suspended once his green identity becomes known. His physician, for example, decides not to honor the confidentiality of the patient-physician relationship.

Moreover, there is a system of *stratification* within Adamsville itself. Skin color, beyond being a prime indicator of one's social standing, signifies as well one's inner spiritual state. Episode 12 clearly reveals the existence and nature of a *minority group* within Adamsville. Knapp and other dull greens in the community experience social segregation and job discrimination, physical abuse, and labeling and stereotyping (they are sometimes referred to as "milk-whites").

It should be apparent at this point that the entire story, which dramatizes the minority status of the mutants in the larger society, not only parallels the actual history of American minorities but also reflects a number of contemporary issues as well. For example, the debate whether greens are human and deserving of civil rights echoes early periods in American history when blacks and Indians were generally considered subhuman. The disruption and violence depicted in Episode 14 has certain parallels with events now taking place in the United States and Ireland.

Often the cultural agreements of minorities are viewed by members of the dominant culture as deviant. The greens' agreement to rescue is a dramatic example of this. Monica's statement in Episode 13 that "kidnapping ought to be wrong in any culture" raises an important issue for reflection. Just because some societies encourage certain kinds of behavior, does it necessarily follow that the behavior is *not* universally evil? Or are there behaviors that should be defined as deviant according to cross-cultural, universal standards? Much of Episode 13 deals with the sociology of deviance. Readers might analyze some of the dialogue in this episode to find out how it illustrates the *labeling, conflict,* and *functionalist* perspectives on deviance. Also, they might attempt to explain what encouraged Gabe to kidnap, using social disorganization theory and/or the concept of differential association as guidelines for the explanation. Finally, they can ask from whose point of view Gabe is deviant or nondeviant and whose perspective, if either, is "correct."

A number of the episodes depict many characteristics of *social change*. Episode 14, for example, includes examples of *conflict* and *collective behavior,* two concepts basic to social change. Charismatic leader Larry Jones heads a conservative (and what some might label *reactionary*) social movement whose purpose is to protect green culture from further change by restoring in Adamsville beliefs and values that have already been modified and by maintaining surviving ones. In his confrontation with the Elders, Larry Jones employs a common tactic for resisting social change—defining the threatened change as a form of deviance that is being promoted by outside agitators.

As Larry Jones sees it, some of the most threatening outside agitators are the three sociologists who, early in the story, were allowed by the Elders to visit and study Adamsville. Ruth Jones permits their visit because she feels that most of outsiders' information about greens gained from journalists is erroneous, much of it based on rumor and hearsay. Information gathered by social scientists promises to be more accurate. Moreover, the Elders want the world to know that greens are "a moral people" and feel that the sociologists can help get this message to nongreens.

The sociologists assure the Elders that their inquiry will be "systematic, logical, and open-minded." Conclusions about morality, green or otherwise, can hardly be drawn from social scientific research, however. The three scientists are aware that they have personal values, but feel confident that they can set these aside in the course of their research.

At the same time, each sociologist embraces a different theoretical perspective that will guide and influence his or her investigation. Constance Batterson, a *conflict theorist,* sees society as divided by class struggle between the powerful and the powerless. Louise Roanoke is a *functionalist.* She is primarily interested in the dynamics of cultural

INTRODUCTION

agreements and whether they are functional—or dysfunctional—to society. Bradley Duncan is a *symbolic interactionist*, bent on studying how Adamsville's cultural agreements emerged and continue to emerge and change.

By Episode 3, Duncan has decided that the best way for him to research greens is to live with them and observe them directly. Sociologists call this research method *participant observation*. Later in the story Duncan writes a scientific paper relating what he has observed and concluded. The paper challenges greens' basic religious beliefs. The scientist's paper sufficiently unsettles enough greens so that Larry Jones can use the issue to mobilize opposition to the Elders' leadership. Duncan's research, however, creates unforeseen difficulties for the Elders, who had invited him into the community in the hope that his research would somehow help them.

This sequence of events points to a larger issue, one that Louise Roanoke ponders late one night in her office. To whom, if anyone, do sociologists owe ultimate allegiance? How much information does the scientist owe the government, particularly when federal grants finance research? What considerations do social scientists owe their subjects, particularly when the interests of their subjects clash with those of the larger society? As the sociologists struggle with these issues, it becomes evident that their presence and research influences and substantially changes the lives of both greens and nongreens. They, too, participate in the construction of social reality.

In addition to the concepts elucidated above, the story illustrates others. In Episode 6, for example, both the positive and negative characteristics of a *bureaucracy* are portrayed. The business of the office of the secretary of the interior continues, uninterrupted by Allen Steinburg's heart attack. On the other hand, the Chicago National Insurance Company appears to be mobilized for work that has long since become unnecessary. In Episode 17, the issue of how technology contributes to—and sometimes determines—cultural change, is explored. It is evident, furthermore, that changes in the social definition of greens will give rise to new technology, which promises to change greens' lives still more.

Sociological concepts particularly depicted in individual episodes are listed at the beginning of the relevant episode. In addition, many concepts (as we have seen) are thematic and are dramatized throughout the story.

Why dramatize sociology through fiction? There are several reasons. Fictionalizing sociological concepts allows the reader to see how sociology (the academic study of society) is related to the daily habits, concerns, and beliefs of real (not hypothetical) people. Fictional dramatization embues intellectual understanding with emotional and imaginative understanding, which in turn facilitates learning, or "getting," sociology.

Because fiction, unlike sociology, focuses on single, personal characters, it also dramatizes how group phenomena affect individuals' lives. Finally, fiction depicts people in the process of making choices and determining their own lives. As a scientific discipline, sociology focuses mainly on human beings as socialized and determined entities. Fiction and sociology together, however, promise a view of human beings as both determined by—and determiners of—social reality.

My final—and perhaps most important—reason for writing *The Story of Adamsville* was to entertain. With that goal in mind, I set about writing an action-oriented, suspenseful tale. I hope you like it.

Cast of Characters

Louise Roanoke Sociologist primarily of the functionalist perspective; at American University, Chicago.

Constance Batterson Sociologist primarily of the conflict perspective; American University.

Bradley Duncan Sociologist primarily of the symbolic interactionist perspective; American University.

Gabriel Knapp Posing green; employed by Chicago National Insurance Company, Chicago.

Monica Roanoke Attorney in the Chicago area.

Larry Jones Charismatic leader of the radical militarists in Adamsville.

Ruth and **Michael Jones** Ruling Elders in Adamsville; the only remaining living children of Adam Jones III.

Jonathan Knapp Gabe's soft parent.

Loretta Larson Gabe's stern parent.

Daniel Adamson Young, not-yet-matured green; sent to visit Gabe at Shore Towers.

Jacob Lockwood Gabe's friend from childhood.

Rebecca Lockwood Jacob's distant cousin; niece of Ruth and Michael Jones.

Ann Sullivan A "dull" or "less" green; Adamsville valley resident.

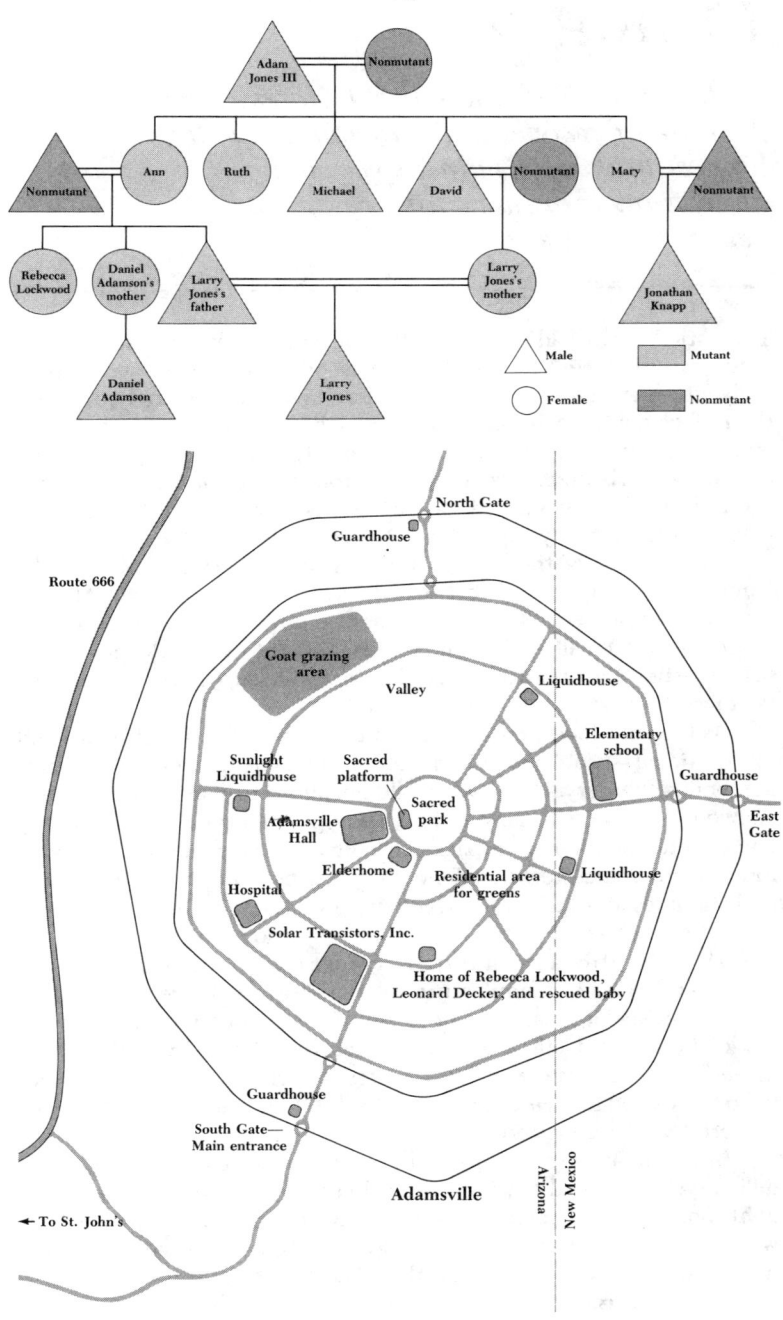

Prologue

By the year 2020 the United States showed promise of recovery. What had been the longest and most painful economic depression in human history had at last begun to weaken.

The entire planet had suffered upheaval. Throughout the final quarter of the twentieth century the Middle East oil cartels had grown increasingly stronger, unmercifully demanding higher and higher prices for their black gold, the lifeblood of industrialized nations. Meanwhile the oil-rich countries, along with other formerly underdeveloped nations, had quickly urbanized. Using energy supplies as rapidly as their Western industrialized clients, these newly modernized countries had accelerated the already rapid depletion of earth's energy reserves.

By the turn of the twenty-first century, a barrel of oil cost the United States fifty times what it had in 1980. Moreover, the Alaskan pipeline had proved a dismal solution. Fraught with labor disputes and engineering difficulties, the pipeline pulsed not even half the oil that had once been anticipated. What the line could supply cost consumers far more than was originally estimated.

As a result, food production had become a serious national—and international—problem. United States farmers needed energy to operate their machinery. Many who could not afford to continue in business allowed their acres to go untilled. They planted what they could by hand, bending their own backs to cultivate their meager harvests, much as their ancestors had done 200 years before. These farmers fed their families, but little was left for those standing in the breadlines of the nation's cities. Americans were hungry and cold.

Then, in 2018, a small corporation located in the Arizona desert announced plans to manufacture solar transistors. Hope returned.

Engineers had made use of solar energy for heating a small number of homes and office buildings since the 1970s. By 1990 nearly three-fourths of those few United States factories still in operation had been converted to solar energy. Also by 1990 some experimental solar-powered vehicles existed.

But solar-powered plants and motor vehicles faced an important difficulty: They could not operate for long periods without direct sunlight. Solar energy could be stored only several hours; during long weeks of haze or overcast skies—and in winter when daylight hours were fewer—solar energy proved an inadequate solution.

Solar transistors (S.T.'s) promised to change all that. Ranging in

Key concept:
Definition of the situation

---

size from that of a dime to an automobile battery, the transistors could emit stored solar energy for up to six months. An S.T. as small as a quarter could, the corporation asserted, heat a small room for several weeks.

With the further development of solar-powered engines and relatively simple conversion procedures, factories and farmers might—it was hoped—resume full capacity. By 2020 Detroit's unemployed looked forward to taking up their positions on the city's assembly lines, where they would fasten bolts in solar-powered vehicles equipped with S.T.'s. Farmers saved what cash they could for down payments on forthcoming S.T.-powered combines. Homemakers dreamed of a return to the affluence of their grandparents: Perhaps one day power companies would use S.T.'s to produce electricity and even dishwashers would hum again.

Renewed hope caused curiosity. Journalists sought interviews with the executives of Solar Transistors, Inc. But requests for interviews were categorically denied. "It is official Policy," S.T., Inc. announced in a national press release, "to deny requests for personal interviews with any S.T.I. personnel and further to deny entrance to S.T.I. property to anyone other than properly identified employees of this corporation."

The press release created a challenge. Competing for the first scoop, free-lance writers, radio and television reporters, and newspaper and magazine journalists struggled frantically for a glimpse inside the revolutionary factory.

Solar Transistors, Inc. still remained shrouded in secrecy. Those few who had by 2019 ordered S.T.'s had done so by mail, they reported. Only one company, a steel producer based in Gary, Indiana, told of personal contact with anyone representing S.T.I. Granting an interview to *Newsweek*, the steel executive described the sales representative who called upon him. "He was polite, cooperative, and well informed," the executive said. "I offered to take him to lunch, but he declined."

On March 10, 2020, Josephine Langley and Robert Parks, reporters for the *Phoenix Herald,* successfully invaded S.T.I. headquarters.

3

Having parked the car in which they approached some distance away, they entered the premises under cover of darkness. Crawling past several armed guards and carrying portable telephones, Parks and Langley tunneled under the fence bordering S.T.I. property and once inside crept almost a mile. They came upon a single-story, glass-roofed building that they correctly supposed to be the corporation's main quarters. Jimmying doors and scurrying tiptoe through the darkened corridors, the two happened upon offices belonging to S.T.I.'s board of directors.

Langley and Parks spent several hours reading, photographing, and telephoning information from S.T.I. files. Receivers at the *Phoenix Herald* picked up the electronically transmitted data.

The corporation, the journalists reported, was owned by a large family or clan, all descendants of a man named Adam Jones III, deceased. While over 625 members owned shares in the corporation, more than half the stock was held jointly by Ruth and Michael Jones, Adam's two living children.

Adam Jones III had purchased 2500 acres along the Arizona-New Mexico border in 1965. He was forty-five years old at the time.

Jones's father, Adam, Jr., had amassed a considerable fortune in the manufacture of small electric home appliances after World War II. When he died in 1950, he left his son, an only child, a substantial inheritance. Adam III, moreover, increased his father's fortune by investing wisely in the stock market.

Adam Jones III had married young and fathered five children, who, in 1965 when he purchased the Arizona-New Mexico property, ranged in age from thirteen to twenty-six. Adam's wife had divorced him in 1964. Jones had apparently gained custody of their minor children, and during 1966—records showed—he built on the desert property a large home for himself, his children, and "any future posterity."

Ann, Jones's eldest descendant, had married at age seventeen and was herself divorced eight years later. She had borne four children and in 1966 she returned with the children to her father's home. By 1970 all five of Jones's children and at least eleven grandchildren had joined him. Parks and Langley found no record of the presence of Jones's children's spouses at the estate.

In 1971 Mary, Adam's youngest daughter, then nineteen, and her older brother, David, thirty, were brutally beaten by hoodlums as they attended a movie in nearby St. Johns, Arizona. Mary was pronounced dead on arrival at a Tucson hospital. David died within the following week, leaving three children.

Shortly after the incident Adam installed an electric fence around the whole property, positioned family members as guards near the three entrances, and began to insist that those residing on the estate

THE STORY OF ADAMSVILLE

remain within its boundaries whenever possible. After that, it appeared, the Jones clan became increasingly secretive. While the family's youth often left to attend colleges and universities, they were strongly encouraged to return before their twenty-sixth birthdays and thereafter to remain upon Jones's territory.

One further incident increased Adam Jones's determined attempts to shield his family from the rest of the world. In 1980 his daughter Ann, while standing guard duty, was fatally wounded by a shot from an outsider's high-powered rifle.

In 1985 Jones's grandchildren were growing up, and according to records that Parks and Langley discovered, some had intermarried rather than seeking mates outside the estate. By 2000, the year of Adam's death, the property sheltered some 250 people. That number had increased to over 575 by 2018.

Adam Jones had educated his children in the best American universities. While still in graduate school, Adam's son Michael had demonstrated promise in the field of electronics. Upon his subsequent return to his father's estate, he had begun to experiment with solar radiation. Michael's older sister Ruth, herself an engineer, had collaborated in these early experiments.

In 2005 the pair received a $500,000 federal grant from the Energy Resources Development Administration (ERDA). The money was to aid private industry in the development of new energy resources.

It appeared, Parks and Langley transmitted, that neither Ruth nor Michael had dealt personally, however, with anyone from the United States government. According to the records David Jones's grandson, Larry, then twenty-one, had made several trips to Washington, D.C., during 2004. Apparently it was Larry who convinced ERDA of his family's potential for successfully harnessing solar energy.

The thirteen years between 2005 and 2018 were spent in secluded research. Again and again, minutes of S.T.I. board meetings revealed, members considered means for ensuring absolute secrecy. It had become important to the family that they be the first—and only—producers of solar transistors.

Moreover, Larry—board member along with Ruth and Michael—often urged stronger measures for the family's defense. In 2015, records showed, Larry was successful in persuading the corporation to set aside a substantial portion of its annual budget for the development of "a complete solar weapons system."

Two years later the family had begun testing a solar laser that would, when perfected, beam death to "any potential enemy within a 10-mile radius." Also by that time the corporation had initiated the design of solar shields, future defense weapons.

But the primary interest of S.T.I. remained in creating a device for solar energy storage. In 2018, in a mailed press release to the *New York Times*, the corporation publicly announced its success.

Faced with the need to market its solar transistors, the family permitted a handful of its young members to leave the estate in order to act as sales representatives. By 2020, the journalists transmitted, the corporation employed five such representatives, all between twenty and twenty-four years of age.

● ● ●

What happened shortly after 4 A.M., the morning of March 11, 2020, is not exactly clear. Langley whispered into her transmitter, "Someone's coming." After a short pause she gasped one additional sentence. That sentence was followed by what sounded at the *Phoenix Herald* like a scuffle. Minutes later a male voice—probably that of Parks—stuttered a frightened, "We'll get back to you." An abrupt click followed, after which all transmission ceased.

At 5:30 A.M. March 11, the car in which Parks and Langley were returning to Phoenix left the road, striking a power pole. The accident proved instantly fatal to both. Subsequent investigation by the Arizona state police revealed that the driver was speeding and had lost control of the vehicle.

On March 12, 2020, the *Phoenix Herald* issued a special edition. Across its front page the paper ran the following headline:

TWO REPORTERS KILLED;
THEIR FINAL STORY:
S.T.I. DIRECTORS ARE GREEN!

● ● ●

"Greens" had appeared on earth. The beings resembled humans except that their skin color took on an increasingly green cast as they approached their late twenties. In 2024 biochemists, working with what data they could uncover, reported the creatures could photosynthesize. The mossy flesh tone, these scientists asserted, was due to the presence of chlorophyll within epidermal cells.

While no one could state with certainty the causes for the mutation, some evolutionary scientists theorized that it was a response to the worsening world food shortage. Others of equal stature argued differently. The mutation, these latter scientists believed, could only be retrogressive: a throwback to an earlier evolutionary period, a reversion to something resembling plant life.

"We must come to an agreement soon," the president of the United States anxiously admonished his secretary of the interior in

THE STORY OF ADAMSVILLE

February 2026. "The country is going crazy!"

"Sir," Secretary Steinburg began.

"It's six years now," the president interrupted, "since those two reporters turned this country upside down. What we've got is bedlam. Half the people want greens executed. 'We can't live with monsters,' they're screaming. The other half say, *'Leave them alone, let them sell us solar transistors, let them ASSIMILATE, for God's sake!'* "

"We do need the energy, sir."

The president paced. "We've spent 400 million dollars," he said quietly, "on espionage directed specifically at greens, and still we can't come up with the formula to manufacture our own S.T.'s." He paused, then slammed his fist on his desk. "Now some crazy liberal group is claiming we've violated the creatures' civil rights!"

"That is a valid issue, Mr. President."

"How do you know that, Steinburg? We can't even be sure they *have* civil rights. We haven't yet decided whether the things are *human.*"

"Sir," Steinburg ventured cautiously, "Are you personally in favor of annihilation?"

"I'm not in favor of anything yet," the president snapped. "Most of these greens don't need to eat. What if they're multiplying in China? In Australia? Suppose Canada has its own green monsters, lets them alone, lets them assimilate. And we kill ours. Then what? Then you've got a country of people who hardly even need to eat living next door to a nation whose people are hungry. Hungry, Steinburg." He repeated the word for emphasis. "Then what happens? Canada could stockpile a grain surplus while we would be experiencing a shortage. That would put Canada in a position to demand exorbitant prices for their surplus food."

"So maybe we need the greens. Is that what you're saying?"

The president sat behind his desk. "Sit down," he said.

Steinburg slid into a chair and faced the president from across the desk.

The chief executive leaned forward. "The CIA report came in this morning. It's classified 'top secret.'" The president paused. "Steinburg," he said finally, "greens have working solar weapons—a solar laser and defense shields."

The secretary stared in silence. "What kind of creatures *are* these?" he whispered.

The president's voice was unusually loud. "I'm saying find out, Steinburg. FIND OUT!"

Episode 2

"They photosynthesize, ladies and gentlemen. Our problem, simply put, is to define them."

The date was May 15, 2026. In Washington, D.C., United States Secretary of the Interior Allen Steinburg was opening the first National Conference on Human Mutations.

Dr. Louise Roanoke, forty, single, internationally known sociologist, listened, intent. She had flown from Chicago in order to address the conference later that afternoon.

"We must know," the secretary pursued dramatically, "what these creatures are. Are they human mutants? It would appear so. Are they then ultimately beneficial to humankind—or harmful throwbacks bent on taking over civilization? Esteemed scientists, are they humans or monsters?"

Steinburg wiped his forehead and took his seat. It had been done, just as the president had ordered: Two hundred of the world's top behavioral, natural, and physical scientists were marshaled to solve what appeared to be one of the most pressing national—and human—problems since the beginning of the species.

Now Dr. Roanoke exchanged glances with a fellow sociologist, Dr. Constance Batterson.

"Nervous?" the latter mouthed from across the room. Roanoke nodded.

Speaking was an American historian who had been researching greens since the turn of the twenty-first century.

"The first green mutant, Adam Jones III," he read from his notes, "had been living in Phoenix as a recluse from the time he was twenty-six because he could no longer pass as normal. His normal wife, it appears, thought Jones to be suffering from some previously unheard-of disease and remained with him as nurse and companion until 1964, when she divorced him. We do not know the reasons for the divorce. We can hypothesize that Mrs. Jones refused to follow her husband to his newly acquired desert estate.

"Adam Jones's descendants multiplied rapidly. Perhaps to lessen confusion, they had, by the third generation, begun to adopt last names other than 'Jones.'

Key concepts:
Sociological perspective
Conflict theory
Symbolic interaction
Functionalism

"By the year 2025," the historian continued, "mutants in Green Colony numbered close to 800."

Steinburg shifted in his chair. What *were* these things? How was his government to deal with them? What national policies were to be formulated?

The historian had finished. Dr. Charles Turquet, a French psychologist, stood at the podium now. He told the audience that greens were probably just as aggressive as normal humans—but not more so.

Dr. Batterson listened with interest. As a conflict sociologist, she wondered whether aggression levels could be explained successfully from only the psychological point of view. It seemed to her, rather, that people became aggressive when they as a group began to feel that they had been imposed upon by society's more privileged.

Still, argued the psychologists, some members of an underprivileged class react more aggressively than others. That, they emphasized, can be explained by either psychology or social psychology.

Nervously Steinburg lit a cigarette. Soon it was Roanoke's turn to speak. She was a small-boned woman. Her dark hair had begun to gray. She wore it in tight curls close to her face, a style which accented her nicely formed features. Adjusting her glasses, she approached the podium.

"Allow me first," she began, "to introduce two American University sociologists who are equally involved with me in the scientific study of greens. It is by two flips of the proverbial coin that I stand before you now, rather than one of them.

"One of my colleagues is Dr. Constance Batterson. Will you stand please, Connie?"

Batterson stood. Tall, thin, thirty-seven, the woman wore a large-brimmed leather hat over her waist-length hair. She smiled, raising a slender hand in a slight wave toward the audience. Before entering the academic world, Batterson had worked five years as a political cartoonist for the *Washington Post.* Her husband was a free-lance photographer.

Roanoke resumed speaking. "My second colleague—and I would like to ask Brad to stand also—is Dr. Bradley Duncan."

Duncan stood: A man of fifty-six, his hair cropped close according to the fashion of the day, he was married to a computer programmer. A symbolic interactionist, Brad was interested in studying how Green Colony's values, beliefs, and norms had emerged—and continued to emerge. He smiled now, bowing almost imperceptibly. He was a person who felt more at ease having a beer with students after an evening class than attending a symposium such as this. Momentarily, Roanoke caught Duncan's eyes. The latter winked his support.

"Now let me tell you," Dr. Roanoke continued, "what we have learned so far—and what we are aiming to learn—about the sociology of greens.

"I must first admit that what we have learned so far is minimal. We have many questions and few answers."

Steinburg winced. How long could the government wait?

"A green mutant, ladies and gentlemen, looks exactly like an average olive-skinned Caucasian from birth until approximately age twenty-five. Greens' respiratory, circulatory, reproductive, and nervous systems appear virtually equivalent to those of normal humans. Their digestive and excretory systems, while capable of reducing food, are probably somewhat atrophied.

"Some greens, we think, remain normal in appearance until they reach thirty. Gradually, however, as mutants age, the chlorophyll within their skin becomes more pronounced in hue. Why the skin is not green at birth is not within the realm of sociology; biochemists are presently at work on that question.

"What is important to the sociological perspective is that greens appear normal for a significant number of years after their birth. We have hypothesized that many during the latter part of this normal period choose to pass; that is, they attend schools, become employed, and perhaps even vote in mass society."

Roanoke paused.

"At the same time we have not one recent reported incidence of any green mutant living among normal humans once he or she has begun to bear evidence of the mutation. This raises a myriad of sociological questions. How and precisely why is it that chlorophyllics are forced from normal society? Or are they? Where do they go once they have 'turned', so to speak?

"Our hypothesis is that they return to Green Colony—or some such other community that we do not know of yet.

"We are, if our hypotheses are correct, presented therefore with a society whose young people move out at some early age, then return as young adults. When and whom do these greens marry? Do they marry? What of their children? Do they marry normals? If so, what happens to these marriages?

"What functions do greens perform once they return to the colony? How does the colony prepare for their return? How do they support themselves? In what manner are they socialized before they first remove themselves from the colony?

"What rules for personal and social conduct have chlorophyllics established? Do they have religion? If so, of what nature is it? How does it function to serve their psychological and social needs?

"What types of political and economic institutions exist in Green Colony? Is there evidence of social stratification within the community itself? Where would greens find themselves within the social stratification system in our present national society?"

Louise paused.

"As a functionalist," she resumed, "I see Green Colony as a social system. I am interested in the community's interrelated parts—how they work together, how they influence and support one another. In what ways does the social institution of family in Green Colony, for example, support the community's social institution of religion or government?"

Dr. Roanoke adjusted her glasses.

"As you can readily see, fellow scientists, we have many, many questions, a few hypotheses, a tremendous need for data—but virtually no answers."

Roanoke paused. "Now I would like to make," she said, "what my colleagues and I feel to be a startling and exciting announcement. Just yesterday, the three of us were granted official permission from Green Colony leaders to visit their community."

The crowd buzzed at this revelation.

"The visit will take place during the week of June 26 of this year. Particular arrangements are yet to be made. As I said, we have many questions. I can only predict that when the answers do come, many of them will surprise us."

* * *

On June 25, 2026, in Chicago, Illinois, Gabriel Knapp, thirty-two, carefully locked the door to his private office and reread a physician's report. It had been an excruciating physical. He should never have agreed to it, he reprimanded himself, in spite of a new company policy that required executives to undergo thorough medical examinations every five years.

Gabriel's eyes snagged at salient terms and phrases: abnormal metabolic rate, chemical imbalance, chlorophyll.

He buzzed his secretary. "Mr. Jacobs," he said, "I'm going to be out of the office this afternoon. Something's come up. If anyone calls, take care of it, will you?"

Fifteen minutes later Gabriel Knapp exited the Chicago National Insurance building on Michigan Avenue, the medical report tucked safely under his arm. He would go home to think.

He walked the several blocks to Shore Towers, a high-rise apartment complex on Lake Shore Drive. It was a plush structure, and, as he approached the familiar uniformed doorman, Gabe felt pleased that he could live so well in times like these. The Great Depression had made Americans more security-conscious than they had been. As a result, the insurance business remained relatively stable.

When he had entered his apartment, Gabe made himself a cup of coffee and removed his suit coat and shirt. He walked out onto the terrace. There he could stand in the late afternoon sunlight.

"Now you have to think," he told himself. "Think." He placed his fingers near the top of his forehead, then moved them back across his skull, absently parting his thick black hair. He could burn the report, inform the board of directors that it had been lost. There was a chance they would not pursue the matter.

Perhaps he should hire Monica to represent him. An attorney, she could argue in court that the company had no right to demand such personal information of its employees. But, he considered, whether he won or not, his favorable position at Chicago National would surely be jeopardized. A lawyer was not the answer.

He might make an appointment with Hopkins, president of the company, and tell her the truth. Explain to her that it was probably no problem, that he was thirty-two years old now and had not experienced any changes whatsoever, that he expected the mutation might never become glaringly noticeable. He was in a position now, he would argue, where his experience in and knowledge of the insurance industry were valuable. It would be foolish of the company to let him go. And anyway, this was only a medical report, only something different going on in his metabolism—something no one could see.

Gabe lit a cigarette—a habit he had formed recently—and made himself another cup of coffee. He placed the report in a secret compartment of his briefcase. Burning it, he realized, would do no good. There would be questions—another physical perhaps. It would all come out eventually anyway. He had known—and tried not to know —that for several years now.

The phone rang.

"Gabe? Larry Jones here. I called your office and they said you were out for the afternoon, so I thought I'd try you at home."

"I can't talk now, Larry."

"Well, you'd better; it's important. This won't take long. I'm on long distance."

"Larry, please. Not now."

"Listen. There's a boy baby, Leonard Decker's son, in Lake Hospital there. Born this morning. We can trace his lineage back to Adam."

"Larry, I can't. Not now."

"You're the only one who can do this assignment, Gabe. There are no other posers available in the lake area. Everything's in order."

Gabe's tone became anxious. "I've got problems here myself," he said.

"That's tough, Gabe. You're overdue anyway and you know it. They're getting angry here. Now listen: You get the baby and this Wednesday, June 28, you fly with him to Phoenix. U.S.-Russian Airlines non-stop out of Chicago, 2:40 P.M., flight 742. Someone will be there to meet you."

Gabe replaced the receiver, then picked it up again and dialed. Once Chicago National executives read the medical report, the thought came to him, they would get suspicious. Begin investigating. Find out the rest.

"I'd like to speak with Monica Roanoke," he was saying.

"Ms. Roanoke is with a client. May I ask who's calling, please?"

"Gabe Knapp. Tell her it's important."

"I'm sorry, Gabe," came the receptionist's response. "I didn't recognize your voice. I'll ring her."

Gabe waited. "Monica," he said finally, "I have to see you. Would you come over here after work? It's really important."

Episode 3

Gabriel Knapp flipped a switch. The custom-installed fluorescent tubes above his bed receded and were subsequently hidden by a false ceiling. Monica would arrive soon.

He dressed, examining himself as he had done methodically for the past eight years. The evidence had been located, he thought, through medical technology. It was only a matter of time now.

More than three years ago Gabe had conceived the private hope that he was somehow to escape his future, that perhaps—in spite of all he knew to be true—he was not one of Adam's people.

He couldn't help feeling bitter now. Seven years ago, he mused, he had been ready. Prepared to return. Anxious for maturity. Anxious even in spite of the fact that his skin showed little promise of becoming true green and that, as a result, his status at home would never equal that of greens like Larry Jones or Rebecca Lockwood.

But today? Today there was the private executive office at Chicago National. Today there was the Lake Shore apartment. Today there was Monica. He was thirty-two years old now, he mused, and had lived more than one-third of his life on the outside. He had made friends here, made a home here. He had told no one of his mutation.

"What's wrong?" Monica was saying as she arrived.

"Nothing."

"Well, it must be *something*. You sounded awful on the phone this afternoon."

Gabe fixed two drinks.

"What *is* it?" Monica whispered finally. "You're staring."

"I just needed to talk to you." Silently he sipped his drink. Whatever he had wanted to talk about, Monica realized, he was having difficulty approaching it now.

"Say," she changed her tone. "The firm's planning a big deal for July Fourth—picnic, fireworks—they're even splurging for real beefsteaks. Want to go?"

"I might have to be out of town."

"Where's the insurance industry sending you this time?"

"Phoenix." He shifted. "But maybe I'll be back by the Fourth. When do you have to know?"

"At least half an hour before I pick you up."

14

Key concepts:
Scientific investigation/research
Participant observation

He was lucky, he thought. She gave him room, didn't pressure.

They had discussed marriage once. It had been he who initiated the conversation. How foolish, he grimaced now, even to dream that his mutation might remain secret.

Anyway, the discussion had not gone well. Monica had surprised him. "I think I'd like to have children right away," she had blithely announced.

"Right away?" He was incredulous.

"Why not?"

"We've got our careers now," he explained calmly. "We'll concentrate on our careers for the next few years, and then we'll raise children."

"Well," Monica was playing now, "what if I get pregnant on our wedding night?"

"We'd give it away," Gabe had responded automatically without reflection.

Monica's chin dropped. "Gabriel," she breathed, "that's a horrid joke."

The conversation had occurred several months before. Now Gabe gazed at Monica. Slowly he was beginning to realize that someday he would have to tell her exactly who he was.

"Monica," Gabriel asked, "how about another drink?"

● ● ●

Batterson, Duncan, and Roanoke departed American University in Chicago and landed in Phoenix early the next morning, June 28, 2026. There they rented a car and drove toward Green Colony.

Located in a sparsely populated area of the Arizona-New Mexico desert, the community proved difficult to find. The trio had driven within what they knew to be the general vicinity of Green Colony for some hours before they were stopped by an armed guard. A wrought-iron gate bearing the sign "Adamsville" curved across a narrow, unpaved road.

"May I help you?" asked the female attendant. She was young, Duncan noted, and scantily attired for such an "official" position. Her hair was long, bleached from overexposure to a blistering sun. Her skin was like that of a nonmutant. She carried a rifle.

"We are looking for Green Colony," Duncan offered from his position in the driver's seat.

"There is no Green Colony here," came the terse reply.

Roanoke leaned across Duncan. "We are looking for a colony of mutants that we know to be located somewhere near here."

"This is private property," the woman said. "No one is admitted without official documents."

"We have with us a letter from a Michael Jones-the-Elder," Duncan responded quickly, pulling the briefcase which contained the letter into his lap. He passed it to the guard. The letter granted permission for a two-hour interview. The team was expected to depart the community by 2 P.M. that day, the communication read.

"I will have to phone ahead," she said. She walked toward a small, glass-roofed booth near the edge of the road. When the guard returned, she announced with noticeable surprise, "You have received clearance to the next gate."

At a second gate, the team was greeted by a woman in her fifties, her skin a dark emerald.

"I am Rebecca Lockwood," she introduced herself. "I will take you to the home of my forebears." Without invitation she opened the rear door of the sociologists' rented auto and slid into the seat behind the three visitors. "If you will just drive slowly ahead," she began, "we will soon be in town. From there I will direct you to Elderhome."

"Elderhome?" Roanoke repeated.

"The home of Adamsville's two remaining elders."

"Has Green Colony always been your home?" Constance asked, turning slightly from her position in the front seat.

"There is no Green Colony," Rebecca Lockwood answered firmly. "The name of the community is Adamsville. Outsiders have written about 'Green Colony' for several years now. But there is no such place."

"What you're implying," Duncan suggested, "is that while outsiders—scientists, politicians, journalists—have chosen to call your community 'Green Colony', the folks here do not accept that name."

"There is no such thing as 'Green Colony'," the woman repeated. "There is only Adamsville, named by my grandfather shortly after he established the community."

The vehicle approached the center of the colony.

The town was small. A spacious park occupied what appeared to be the hub of the miniature city. Adjacent to the park stood a modern, single-story building of adobe and glass. This was Elderhome.

"Turn left and stop just ahead," Lockwood directed.

After Duncan parked the car, the four stepped out into the glaring desert sun.

"My uncle and aunt will have finished noon light-break shortly," Lockwood advised. "Then they will see you. Meanwhile, I shall show you into the Elderhome parlor."

As the party entered the adobe structure, Duncan noted the clean, uncluttered lines of the architecture.

"Won't you be seated?" Lockwood suggested. "Allow me to offer you some refreshment," she added politely, pushing a button on a wall panel behind her. The roof receded, and the three felt pierced by the sharp sunlight.

"Make yourself comfortable," Lockwood said. "The elders will be here shortly."

Connie Batterson yearned for her sunglasses. Duncan wiped his brow. Finally two persons, advanced in age, entered the room. Their green skin dazzled.

"I presume you are the sociologists from American University," the female began. "I am Ruth Jones, the eldest living of Adam's children. This is my brother, Michael. Together we govern Adamsville."

As the party walked to the glass-enclosed "ruling center," the sociologists introduced themselves. Once in the official administrative office, Michael and Ruth took their places behind a long table. They faced their guests who sat in comfortable chairs along the other side of the table.

"Now," Ruth began, "I want to be brief and to the point. This is an important day in the history of Adamsville. It is the first time that we have responded favorably to a request from outsiders to enter our community. We have done so for two reasons: First, we know that information on the colony is leaking to the outside. That leaked information is not always correct. Often it is gathered haphazardly. Someone sneaks in, talks to one or two of us maybe, and goes off. The resulting information is often biased. By the time the story gets into the newspapers, it may be grossly inaccurate.

"We figure it is time, since information is leaking out anyway, to allow people here who will gather the facts systematically and report what they see without bias.

"The second reason we have allowed you here," Ruth continued, "is that we believe what you discover may help us. We are beginning to experience a serious problem. Some of our young people are not fulfilling their obligations to the community. They lack loyalty. We want to know why."

The five talked at length.

"How can you be sure that what you find will be accurate?" Michael challenged the sociologists.

"We can't," Duncan said. "We can only be reasonably certain. And we can promise that we will strive to be systematic, logical, and open-minded. We will not jump to conclusions."

"We do not pretend to have come here without personal values," Constance said. "But as scientists we can try to recognize these values. Then, aware of them, we will not unconsciously let them influence either our observation or analysis."

"I must explain," Michael said, "that some factions within the community are not in favor of your being here. They resent being studied. They feel their privacy is a sacred thing, not to be infringed upon. You cannot expect cooperation from every member of this community."

"Some fear your being here," Ruth added. "They feel that it is best for us to remain living in complete secrecy. They trace the beginnings of many of our community's troubles to the invasion by those two reporters six years ago. They feel that the more the world knows about us, the more endangered we become. Sometimes outsiders picket our gates. They carry signs that say horrible things, like 'KILL THE GREEN MONSTERS'. We never experienced that before ungreens came poking around."

"How do you answer your dissenters?" Louise asked.

"We believe," Michael said, "that the outside must be told who we are. We are the saviors of the world, a new people, the fathers and mothers of a new humanity. The world cannot survive without us. Once people realize this, we will be accepted."

"Indeed," Ruth said, "we will be more than accepted. The earth will be ours."

Batterson and Roanoke exchanged glances.

"But we must know," Ruth shifted the focus of the conversation, "how you plan to gather your information."

Duncan responded. "I would like to be allowed to return," he said, somewhat hesitantly, "to live here for a time with your people, to participate as well as I can in the lives of your people."

"Why?" Ruth demanded.

"It is one of the best ways I know," he said, "to practice social science."

"We can arrange that," Michael replied. "Some will think it an unwise decision, but Ruth and I are convinced otherwise. We are moral people and we want outsiders to understand that. Nothing ill can come of the truth."

Ruth sat quiet a moment, apparently engaged in heavy thought.

"This afternoon," she said suddenly, "the community will have a welcoming ceremony. According to our previous plans, you were to have left Adamsville before the ceremony began. But we would like you all to stay for the welcoming. You will enjoy it. It is a wonderful celebration."

Michael Jones-the-Elder pushed a button on the table in front of him. A gentleman of forty, his complexion the color of fresh limes, entered the room.

"Mr. Alexander," Jones announced, "these people are guests of Ruth and myself. They have been invited to attend the ceremony this afternoon. Please escort them. You will be their host."

The man nodded. "Come with me," he said.

Episode 4

The weather was dismal in Chicago Wednesday, June 28. It had rained for several days, and the morning forecast offered no hope for early change.

Gabe stood on Lake Shore Drive, the wind beating beads of water into his neck and face. Tugging at his jacket collar, he tried to hail one of the city's fewer and fewer cabs. In his left hand he carried a small brown suitcase. He kept his head lowered, in defense against the stinging rain and also to lessen his chances of being recognized.

He had called in sick to Chicago National, complaining of a summer cold. He had told Monica he must leave town on business. He would not risk being recognized.

A taxi stopped. "Lake Hospital," Gabe announced abruptly, sliding into the back seat, his head lowered. Hidden beneath his jacket was a sling used to carry very young babies.

Once in the hospital lobby, Gabe located a rest room. He entered, locked himself inside a toilet stall, and opened the suitcase. He pulled a mustache from the case, positioned it above his lip. He smoothed a light-brown wig over his own dark hair. He removed the blue jacket he had been wearing and replaced it with a tan one. Having stuffed the blue jacket into a waste bin, he closed the suitcase and left the rest room.

At a flower stand in the lobby he purchased a bouquet. Near the elevator door he scanned the directory posted on the wall. "Maternity," he read, "2." Gabe entered the elevator and pushed the button for the second floor.

"Suppose you get caught," he asked himself repeatedly as he had done since the night Larry called. The elevator door opened; Gabe was on the second floor.

A nurse approached. "You look lost," he smiled. "May I help you?"

"My wife just had a baby," Gabe said. "I haven't seen him yet. Which way is the nursery?"

"Congratulations," came the response. "Just down the hall to your left."

Gabe walked along the hall that the nurse had designated. When he approached the windowed nursery, he observed a nurse attending the infants. He noted the closed door into the room and positioned himself so that he could peer through the glass window and also stand as near as possible to the door.

Key concepts:
Culture
Subculture
Ethnocentrism
In-group/out-group

He scanned the identification tags at the foot of each bassinet. In the row nearest him he spotted what he was looking for: "Decker," the tag read, "male; 7 pounds, 5 ounces."

"And he's near the door," Gabe thought. "This was meant to be."

Gabe turned, searching for a stairwell. He knew there had to be one; it was mandatory due to fire regulations. At the end of the hallway he spotted a metal door, marked "EXIT." Casually he walked toward it, opened it, saw that it led to a stairway and that the stairway exited onto an outside street two flights below. He returned to his previous position at the nursery window.

The attendant had begun systematically to change diapers. She began at the far side of the room and, as Gabe watched for several minutes, he noted that often, for as many as ninety seconds, the attendant's back was turned toward him. It would be possible, he considered, to open the door, grab the Decker child, and escape down the back stairway without being seen. If the attendant continued to work systematically around the room, she would not look directly into the Decker crib for almost fifteen minutes.

Gabe waited. Again he counted the seconds during which the nurse kept her back to him.

The attendant finished changing a baby, patted it on the bottom, and moved to the next. "It's time now," Gabe told himself. "Do it."

Slowly he opened the door. Tiptoeing into the room, he scooped up the Decker infant, placed his hand over its tiny mouth so as to muffle a possible wail, and moved quickly from the room.

Once in the hall he dropped the freshly cut flowers into a drinking fountain and dashed toward the stairway. In the sling over his left shoulder Gabe smuggled the baby, partially hidden under his jacket. In his right hand he clutched the suitcase.

Gabe entered the enclosed fire stairway and hurried down the steps. He was unconcerned now with the infant's crying; he would be on the street in seconds.

He shoved through a heavy, metal door to the outside. It was still raining. Unseen, Gabe darted across the street into the rear rest room of a deteriorating service station, locking the door behind him. There he removed the mustache and flushed it down the toilet. He jerked the wig from his head, opened the suitcase, and carefully set the baby down on a brown sweater which he had earlier crumpled inside it. His arms free now, he lifted the cover from the toilet tank and removed the tan jacket he was wearing. He stuffed the jacket and wig into the toilet tank, stepping aside so that the dispersed water, spilling onto the grimy floor, would not soak his shoes. With one foot he gently shoved the suitcase aside so that it would not be wet by the overflow from the tank.

Gabe reached into his pocket and found a comb. Squatting to peer into the small, cloudy mirror which hung precariously on the wall, he combed his hair.

The baby had begun to cry. He picked it up and soothed it. From the suitcase he pulled a baby bottle filled with milk and offered it to the child. Still holding the infant, Gabe later pulled the sweater from the suitcase and put it on.

He knelt beside the open suitcase, balancing the quieted infant upon his knees. From the suitcase he pulled a flannel blanket and a heavier one of waterproof material. He wrapped the baby in the flannel comforter, then folded the bundle into the waterproof shield. He took a pacifier from the suitcase and placed it in the baby's mouth.

Gabe reclosed the case and stood, replacing the child in the sling against his shoulder. With his right hand he pulled several paper towels from a dispenser and wiped his fingerprints from the handle of the emptied case. Then with his foot he wedged it between the toilet stool and the rest-room wall. Gabe shoved open the door and with the infant walked outside.

Again on the street, Gabe boarded a bus to Shore Towers, using the parking garage elevator to get to his apartment. There he changed into a gray business suit. He diapered the infant, then laid it on his bed under the glare of the fluorescent tubes. "You'll feel better shortly," he soothed, "I promise."

He poured himself a cup of coffee. "Damn rain," he said to himself, lighting a cigarette and then immediately extinguishing it.

He returned to the bedroom. The baby had fallen asleep. "We've got to go," he said quietly, working his arms into the sleeves of a full-length raincoat. Gently he scooped up the sleeping seven pounds.

Outside Gabe quickly walked several blocks toward a Loop hotel. The rain was coming down harder now, and Gabe shielded the infant beneath his raincoat. In front of the hotel the two boarded a bus for the airport.

Seated toward the rear, Gabe looked closely into the infant's vulnerable face, then leaned to kiss its forehead. "Soon," he said, "everything will be okay. In just a few hours you'll be home."

THE STORY OF ADAMSVILLE

○ ● ○

The three sociologists followed their guide through a glass-enclosed walkway to a waiting solarmobile. "We do not encourage visitors from the outside." Alexander's tone was cold. He opened the rear door of the readied vehicle. "Consequently," he said, "we have not developed official methods for hospitality. I'm sure you understand."

"Of course," Batterson smiled.

Roanoke settled herself in the solar auto and checked her watch. It was 2:30 P.M. Already, she thought, her colleagues and she had had a long day.

Duncan wiped his forehead. He was hot and hungry. "Excuse me," he leaned forward to address Alexander. "Is there any place near where we might get something to eat? I'm afraid," he added with a forced chuckle, "it's past our lunchtime."

"There are no restaurants in Adamsville," Alexander responded.

"No restaurants?" Batterson asked.

"Eating is a weakness," Alexander said. "To go to restaurants after maturity is against the law."

The vehicle swerved through the small community. Glass sun decks protruded from the west and south sides of each residence. "I'll take you to a liquidhouse."

Sunlight Liquidhouse resembled a tavern. A bartender stood behind a counter. A man of about forty, his skin was moderately green. A large jar of mineral tablets rested on the bar behind him.

"Jake," Alexander said as the four entered, "these ungreens are invited guests of Ruth and Michael. We thought maybe we could get a drink before you close up for the welcoming."

Jake stared. It was apparent he had known nothing of the outsiders' expected visit. He filled four glasses, garnished the drinks with sprigs of parsley, then set the refreshments on the bar. "You're not taking them to the ceremony?" he asked Alexander, incredulous.

Alexander nodded. "On order from Elderhome," he said.

"What are you serving today?" Batterson asked the bartender in an appreciative voice.

"Water. That's mostly all the people want. Liquidhouse down the way a block or so serves coffee now. Young folks got the notion they like coffee."

"Well, it's got to be the best water I've tasted," Batterson said. "That sun is vicious."

Jake stared at the three ungreens. Alexander shuffled. He seemed embarrassed, anxious. It was as if Batterson had committed blasphemy.

"Well, Jake, see you at the ceremony." Alexander set his glass on the counter and turned to exit. Three somewhat confused sociologists followed.

The ceremony was to take place in the park. A crowd had gathered. Alexander escorted the three toward an elevated platform near the edge of the park.

Sparked by scientific curiosity, Batterson decided that she must ask as many questions of her host as he would allow.

"What kind of ceremony will we see today?" she began.

"A welcoming ceremony."

She could see his answers were going to be brief. "Does Adamsville have welcoming ceremonies often?" she pursued.

"We hold the welcoming ceremony whenever it is appropriate," Alexander replied.

"What is a welcoming ceremony?" inquired Roanoke.

"We are welcoming a green infant," Alexander answered.

"Do you have this ceremony whenever a green is born?" asked Duncan, expecting an affirmative answer.

"No," said their host. "Only when the infant has been rescued from the outside."

"Who bore the infant?" asked Batterson.

"It is not important who bore the infant." Alexander turned his back to the triad.

Batterson was unwilling to curtail her inquiry. "We've noticed," she said after a brief silence, "that Adamsville residents are many shades of green. Why is that?"

"Our children do not look green. The mature citizens of Adamsville look green," Alexander answered.

"But even among the adults," Duncan interjected, "some are very green while others show almost no evidence of chlorophyll in their skin."

"A green is a green, Mr. Duncan. I have difficulty answering your question."

The four stayed away from the center of the crowd. Nearer the platform about thirty mutants lay on the ground, as if sunbathing.

"The ceremony will begin when our rescuer arrives," stated Alexander. "We will wait here quietly."

Alexander removed his shoes, socks, and shirt. He positioned himself on the ground, his face projected toward the sun.

The sociologists searched one another's faces. Batterson shivered, in spite of the heat. "What is he doing?" she demanded of her companions. The others shrugged.

"They *are* different shades of green," Roanoke whispered. "Yet Alexander refused to discuss it."

"Perhaps they themselves don't see it," offered Duncan. "It isn't important to them."

"Or they do see it, even more vividly than we do," Batterson offered, "and Alexander simply refuses to share any information with us."

A limousine came to a halt near the expectant crowd. The mutants began to cheer. "Welcome, welcome, welcome," they shouted in unison. "Welcome to your family. Welcome to Adamsville. Welcome to your home."

The shouting, much like a football cheer, went on for several minutes. "Welcome/welcome/welcome," sang the throng. "Welcome to your family/welcome to Adamsville/welcome to your home."

The door of the car opened. Meanwhile Ruth and Michael Jones-the-Elder had appeared in the doorway of their home. Gallantly they proceeded toward the solarmobile. The crowd continued its chant. Ruth ushered from the vehicle a man who was from all appearances not a mutant. He carried in his arms an infant. The three proceeded to the platform.

"From where was this child rescued?" Roanoke asked Alexander.

"From the outside," came the answer.

"Who bore the child?"

"An outsider."

Roanoke cleared her throat. She had forgotten her hunger. "Then the infant is not a green?"

"The infant is a green, the son of a green father."

"Then the infant is half green?" Roanoke pursued hesitantly.

"The infant is green," insisted Alexander. "A green's chromosomes are always dominant. It is right that the infant be raised in Adamsville because he is green."

"Who is the rescuer then?"

Alexander did not reply. The crowd had ceased its chant. All eyes focused on the platform. There the normal-appearing man, evidently the rescuer, stood with the infant still in his arms. He was flanked now by Ruth and Michael Jones.

The rescuer approached the microphone. "I have saved the life of this infant boy," he began the ritualistic litany.

"You have saved the life of this infant boy," returned the crowd.

"Born of green, he is green," the rescuer called.

The crowd repeated the decree.

"Greens, raised outside, die," led the rescuer.

"Greens, raised outside, die," the mass replied.

A stillness ensued. The rescuer placed the infant into the arms of Ruth Jones-the-Elder. A band began to play. Michael Jones approached the microphone.

"Ladies and gentlemen," he said, "we welcome today not only an infant, but a hero. Gabriel Knapp, gone from us for so long, has today demonstrated his loyalty."

The crowd responded with the now-familiar cheer: "Welcome/welcome/welcome..."

Roanoke searched her mind. Gabriel Knapp. The name sounded unnervingly familiar.

Episode 5

Gabriel Knapp was born March 1, 1994, in Nogales, a village along the southern Arizona border. His physical mother was a posing green. Her husband, Gabe's physical father, was Mexican. Gabe remained primarily of his father's complexion and facial characteristics. Yet the chlorophyllic chromosomes of his physical mother had lent an olive cast to his skin.

When Gabe was three months old, his birther noticed that her skin was beginning to turn green. With the aid of two posing rescuers, she fled with the infant to Adamsville. There she contracted the infant to the home of a fellow chlorophyllic, Jonathan Knapp. Gabriel knew nothing of his physical parents. He had never thought to ask. Birthers were, in Adamsville, irrelevant.

Gabriel knew that as a baby he had been rescued from death on the outside. Since a chlorophyllic's chromosomes were always dominant, he was taught only that he had been born a green. Therefore, he had been told from the time he could understand the language of his green parents, it was necessary that he be nurtured as a green.

Furthermore, Gabriel learned early, he owed much to the community that had saved him. The very best thing he might do in appreciation was one day to perform a rescue mission of his own.

And so Gabriel Knapp, from the time he was two years old, had been groomed as a rescuer.

He sat now, July 4, 2026, gazing into Lake Michigan. He had accepted Monica's invitation to her firm's holiday picnic. It had turned into an extravagant yet comfortably casual affair at the lakeside home of one of the firm's senior partners.

Behind Gabe as he stared across the water—but much within his memory—was Lake Hospital. The nongreens around him buzzed over the recent kidnapping, their angry tones pendulum-swinging between disbelief and fear.

Monica Roanoke, sitting beside Gabe, was twenty-eight years old. A year ago she had graduated fifth in her class from the University of Detroit Law School. Today she sought in vain to gain the attention of

Key concepts:
Socialization
Internalization
Role conflict

---

her preoccupied escort. "Gabe," she asked, "would you like to join the egg toss?"

"Not now," he mumbled apologetically. His thoughts wound back to a game *he* had played all through childhood.

Rescue was the equivalent of cops-and-robbers or cowboys-and-Indians in Adamsville. Children ducked in and out of alleys, galloped up staircases, banged screen doors, and upset trash cans. "I have a baby," one would call. "I have a green baby!"

"Come back, come back," another would chant. "It's mine, it's mine."

"No, no, no, no. It isn't yours," the retort might ring. "It's Adam's. Adam wants his green baby!"

Gabriel had played all the parts. When very young, he had been cast in the role of rescued infant. "You were *really* rescued, Gabriel," the little girl down the street had reminded him. "You be the baby."

And Gabriel would pretend to cry. "I want Adamsville," he would wail. "I want to go home."

As Gabe grew older, he played rescuer. Sometimes he carried a toy pistol, sometimes a rope, occasionally a handkerchief to quiet a wailing birther. Sometimes he carried no weapon at all. But essentially his role was the same: to snatch the wailing infant to freedom, to dignity, to health, to life, to Adamsville.

Gabriel had occasionally played the birther. Sometimes when he played the birther he chased his playmates, the rescuers. Other times he handed the child over with acquiescence. "This baby is sick," he would say. "You can make him well."

"Gabe," Monica interrupted his reverie, "remember what I promised? Real beef!"

Eating, Gabriel considered, was for these people a social occasion. It appeared they put things into their mouths while in the presence of one another as a way of saying "I like you." He would never get used to that.

Gabe looked around him. One of Monica's fellow attorneys was slicing a watermelon. Several from her secretarial pool sat on a blanket devouring fried chicken. Someone had fired a large open grill. The steaks awaited on a nearby picnic table. Sporadically the crack of fireworks startled him. But in spite of all this, it occurred to Gabriel with glaring realism, the Fourth of July was not, to his way of thinking, a *real* holiday.

"Now Adam's Birthday, that was *something,*" he said to himself, surprised at the pangs of homesickness he was feeling. He would have liked to talk to Monica about Adam's Birthday. He would have liked to tell her about the green velvet costume he was allowed to wear for the first time when he was twelve—and wore on every holiday thereafter until five years ago when he stopped going back. He would have liked to tell her of his tremendous anticipation—when he was in his teens—for the time when he would no longer need the green costume because his own skin would dazzle with more brilliance than any velvet cloak.

Gabriel jerked. This nostalgia was ridiculous. In the years he had not been to Adamsville, Gabe had nearly forgotten Adam's Birthday, nearly forgotten his unquenchable teenage thirst for entrance into Adamsville Hall. He had in recent years chosen *not* to participate in the maturing ceremony. They had invited him. "You are green," they had said. "Your skin is olive now. Come home. Mature."

Gabe had witnessed more than a dozen maturing ceremonies while growing up in Adamsville. The rite marked the passage of a green to chlorophyllic adulthood. Under ordinary circumstances the ceremony took place after the greening of a young mutant's flesh. Usually this occurred following his or her return to the colony after a period of posing. Adamsville residents held that every green should mature both physically and ritualistically. They believed that all chlorophyllics should one day wear skin which dazzled in its greenness.

Often, however, a mutant's flesh became—and remained—only dull green. Occasionally a chlorophyllic's skin evidenced virtually no sign of the mutation. Failure of a green's skin to change color was interpreted as evidence of some inner intellectual or emotional disloyalty to the colony. Hence, those whose skin did not attain its potential brilliance—while they were expected to participate in the maturation rite before their thirtieth birthday—often found themselves the victims of considerable discrimination. Upon their return to Adamsville after a period of posing, these "dull" or "less" greens were denied access to prestigious positions and enjoyed little voice in decision making. They were made constantly aware that, because of their evidenced lack of commitment to Adamsville, they were to be trusted and respected only with reservation.

Consequently Gabe viewed an eventual return to the colony with mixed emotions. While once he had joyfully anticipated becoming a true, brilliant green, he knew now that his flesh would never change. Meanwhile he had become accustomed to and even grown to enjoy many elements of life on the outside.

"Cheer up, Gabe," Monica's secretary was saying, "it's the Fourth of July!"

"Are you all right, Gabe?" Monica questioned. "You haven't seemed the same since your business trip to Phoenix last week."

"I'm fine," he muttered, becoming aware that he was rudely ignoring Monica. "I'm just a little tired. I'm sorry."

What she had said was true, of course. The trip had taken him back to a past he evidently could not shed as readily as he had thought. Since the rescue, he had been haunted by memories from his Adamsville childhood.

"Want to claim a steak?" Monica suggested.

"Sure." Gabe had learned to accept eating much as the commuter accepts fighting rush-hour traffic. If he was to live on the outside, if he was to keep the executive office at Chicago National Insurance, if he was to continue with Monica, then occasional social eating was a fact of life.

Gabriel had, of course, from the time of his rescue, taken "supplements." All green babies received supplement, usually milk. But as the children grew older, they drank milk only within the privacy of their homes—and always with the expectation that one day, probably shortly before their maturity, the practice would no longer be necessary. Supplements were, Gabriel learned early, at worst a sign of weakness or disloyalty, at best a sign of immaturity. "Take your supplement now," his soft parent would say, handing him a glass of goat's milk, "before we go out." "Supplement is a private matter," his stern parent would admonish. "You mustn't speak of it to anyone."

Now as Gabe placed a piece of meat upon the grill, he remembered an incident which occurred when he was nine. He had gone to school one day as usual. But when the class broke at noon for lightbreak, Gabe and four classmates became adventurous.

"Let's not go to light-break," Joey, a ten-year-old, had teased. "Let's go for a walk."

The children had walked quite a way before they approached the

Adamsville gate.

"We'll get in trouble if we go through," Gabriel had hesitated.

"Oh, come on," coaxed a small girl. "The guard's not even looking."

"What's out there anyway?" someone asked.

"Let's go see," Joey urged, slipping around the gate.

The children skipped along a single-lane road, intoxicated by their mischief. Eventually they approached a combination roadside grocery store and gas station.

"Well, what might I do for you?" asked a rotund clerk, girdled in a white butcher apron.

None of the wayward youngsters responded.

"Aren't you in school today?" asked the grocer.

No one answered.

"How about a piece of chocolate?" he offered.

Gabriel reached to meet the grocer's extended hand. He fingered the strange, foil-wrapped rectangle. He had never seen anything like it before.

"Go ahead," encouraged the man, opening one for himself and thrusting it into his mouth.

Each of the children took a piece of candy. Gabriel could still recall, some twenty-three years later, the sensation as the chocolate touched his tongue.

"Good, isn't it?" the grocer had encouraged.

Gabriel wasn't sure.

"Haven't met a kid yet that doesn't like chocolate. Here, want some more?...Go ahead, it's okay....Here, honey, have another piece. Isn't it good?"

The children had departed the strange establishment licking their palms.

"Where were you?" asked their teacher, Mary Colvin, when they returned. Colvin was a mature green of thirty-one who had received her master's degree in elementary education while still posing. "You were not at light-break."

The children were silent.

"Where were you?" she repeated.

"We went for a walk," offered Joey.

"What is that, Gabriel?" the woman asked then, noticing candy smeared on his shirt.

"Chocolate," he said. "A nice man gave it to us. He said it was good."

"And was it good?" questioned the teacher.

"I don't know," Gabriel answered slowly.

"Greens who often disobey," the teacher warned then, sometimes do not fully mature. Their skin stays dull and lifeless."

Gabe was getting a stomachache. "My stomach hurts," he complained.

"Your stomach aches," explained Ms. Colvin, "because you have eaten. You did not enjoy the taste of the chocolate and now it has given you a stomachache. Eating is never enjoyable."

"Eating is never enjoyable," Gabe thought now, as he positioned a sharp knife over his 6-ounce steak.

"Want some more potato salad?" someone asked. "You didn't take much."

◉ ◉ ◉

Louise Roanoke dug into her half of a barbecued chicken.

"More corn on the cob?" Bradley Duncan passed a platter of buttered corn along his backyard picnic table. It would be the last party he would host for these friends and colleagues for a long time. He was scheduled to leave the next morning to begin a period of field experience in Adamsville.

"This sure beats work," laughed Duncan's wife, Alice. "We ought to have July Fourth more often."

"Every couple of weeks, at least," Brad nodded.

"What would you say," Louise Roanoke asked slowly, "is the manifest function of the Adamsville welcoming ceremony?"

"Hey," Connie Batterson interjected, winking toward her spouse, "I promised my husband we wouldn't talk business today."

"Five minutes," Louise promised.

"The manifest function of the welcoming ceremony?" Brad repeated. "To welcome the stolen baby, change his status."

"Change his status how?" asked Alice, a computer programmer by profession.

"From a stolen baby to a green, from an outsider to an insider."

"How about latent functions? What are some possible latent functions of the welcoming ceremony?" Louise pursued.

"Legitimation of the rescue mission," Constance offered. "Positive sanctioning of the rescuer. Socialization."

"Socialization of whom?" Duncan urged.

"Everyone who was there," Connie answered. "Children, adults —everyone. Did you hear them respond to that litany? I mean they *believed* what they were saying."

"Socialization of the rescuer, too, of course," added Brad.

"I surely would like to know where that baby came from," remarked Roanoke.

"Well, I'd say from the headlines you've got a pretty good estimate," offered Batterson's husband, Paul.

"You think the child was kidnapped from Lake Hospital?"

"Makes sense to me," Paul said. "They catch that guy, they'll hang him."

"Aha," laughed Connie, "now doesn't he talk like he's married to a conflict theorist?"

Louise Roanoke had become too serious for humor. "Gabriel Knapp," she mused. "Somehow I feel I've heard that name before."

"Your niece mentioned a Knapp," Brad recalled casually, "last time she was in the office."

Episode 6

Louise Roanoke leaned back in her office chair and sorted through a stack of mail. It was September; American University students buzzed through the halls again.

The school, situated on an artificial island anchored in Lake Michigan, had been constructed during the 1980s—just before the Great Depression. An expansive deck that encircled the floating campus was itself surrounded by the lake. To the west the Chicago skyline erupted, radiant now as the autumn sun began its slow descent.

There was so much to do, Louise worried: lectures to prepare, schedules to juggle, term projects to assign—the letter from the Department of the Interior to answer.

Roanoke straightened in her chair. At least, she decided, she would write next week's lectures before this afternoon. That way she could relax and enjoy herself tonight when she went to Monica's for dinner.

Louise removed several books from the shelf behind her. On a piece of notepaper she began to sketch an outline. But her mind strayed from the emerging lecture. She opened and reread the letter from the Department of the Interior.

The message was dated September 2, 2026. "Dear Dr. Roanoke," Louise read. "As you know, the position of United States secretary of the interior, since Allen Steinburg's untimely heart attack, is being filled by Edmund Slavik.

"Mr. Slavik has asked that I, as chairman for the acquisition of information on greens in the United States, write you.

"According to our files, you are engaged in sociological research on Green Colony. I understand, moreover, that you and two other sociologists were granted entrance to and actually visited Green Colony last June 28.

"As I'm sure you are aware, the level of anxiety in this nation is rising with regard to greens. The Society for the Protection of the Human Race (SPHR)—along with similar groups—is insisting on green extermination. Rumors are spreading nationally that greens, while passing as normals in larger society, are responsible for the rash of infant kidnappings that we have witnessed over the past forty years.

"The recently formed Association for the Prevention of Infant Kidnappings (APIK) threatens to become the modern counterpart of the Ku Klux Klan. Already this group has threatened vigilante 'law

Key concepts:
Bureaucracy
Voluntary associations
Coalitions

---

enforcement' against any green caught trespassing on private property in Arizona and New Mexico.

"I am sure you are aware of our problem: Whether greens are to be protected or prosecuted is a decision that must be reached rationally rather than emotionally. The decision must be based on fact.

"It is Secretary Slavik's sincere hope that some decisions regarding this possibly socially and economically dangerous group can be reached before or during the second National Conference on Human Mutations scheduled for May, 2027.

"It is his more immediate desire that in the meanwhile you relay to him any scientific data you may gather—or have gathered. Sincerely, Robert Grady, Assistant Secretary, United States Department of the Interior."

What Grady had not written in his letter to Roanoke was that the FBI had been gathering information on kidnappings throughout the United States since long before the first conference the previous May.

While there was nothing official to link any kidnappings with Green Colony, some facts suggested a possible relationship. Kidnappings for ransom were understandable, but the infant thefts that had occurred increasingly over the past forty years were different. Never, in some 300 cases, had anyone demanded ransom. In all these cases, whoever had taken the infant apparently had not so much as attempted to contact the parents.

Of the 300 similar cases, 98 percent had been infant thefts from hospital maternity wings. The others were of babies still in their first year, stolen from playpens in their front yards, or from car seats while they awaited the return of their parents from stores. Three babies had been stolen by baby-sitters who had previously solicited their victimized clients.

Eleven parents of kidnapped infants had committed suicide as a result of their loss.

Roanoke reread Grady's letter. How would she respond? One thing she knew: She would like to consult first with Connie and Brad. She missed them. Connie had left three days before for the American Sociological Association annual meeting in New Orleans. She was to

37

present a paper there on her preliminary work in developing a questionnaire to measure animosity toward greens within American society.

Brad had returned to Adamsville and was still there. He had written Louise early in August concerning an article he was preparing for the *American Journal of Sociology,* entitled "Cultural Agreements and Vocabulary."*

Brad's letter to Louise had discussed more than just his forthcoming publication. Some members of Adamsville—Duncan called them "radical militarists"—had begun to stockpile arms and ammunition. Posers were buying the weapons on the outside and carrying them into the colony. This stockpile, along with small-scale solar weapons already existing in Adamsville, constituted a considerable arsenal.

The Elders exercised official control over the solar weaponry developed by the Adamsville corporation, Solar Transistors, Inc. But they remained unaware of the recent smuggling of arms from the outside. Duncan was unclear as to whether the stockpile was intended for use against outsiders or against Elderhome. He supposed both were possibilities: The radical militarists spoke increasingly of their distrust for the Elders and at the same time seemed concerned about threats of physical attack from hostile outside groups.

The Elders, and those who supported them, Brad termed "cooperationists." The essential difference between this group and the radical militarists, Brad wrote, was that the former stressed cooperation with outsiders while the latter insisted upon complete separation and isolation of Adamsville. Radical militarists maintained that total secrecy was necessary to the well-being of the colony and supported establishing an autonomous Green State separate from the United States.

Ironically the cooperationists appeared unaware of the radical militarists' growing strength. They seemed more concerned with a different problem—one they often referred to as a lack of loyalty on the part of some of their youth. Some greens, the Elders complained, were not assuming their full genetic potential. This malady could only be caused by their secret lack of commitment to Adamsville. One green poser, moreover, had delayed returning for the maturation rite until well after his thirtieth birthday. The cooperationists hoped Duncan could tell them why.

Duncan hoped so too, he wrote, but he could not be sure how long the compromisers would exercise authority over the colony. "If and

---

*In that scientific essay Brad had argued that a group's word choice in certain instances can be evidence of broader beliefs, values, and norms. Duncan had contrasted the implicit connotations of several pairs of words: "posing" and "passing," "rescue" and "kidnap," "birther" and "mother," "Adamsville" and "Green Colony."

when the radical militarists gain control of Adamsville," Brad concluded, "you can expect I'll be evicted immediately if not sooner."

Louise put Grady's official communication under a glass paperweight that her niece, Monica, had given her for her thirty-fifth birthday. She would consider her reply again tomorrow.

○ ○ ○

Meanwhile, Gabriel Knapp had gulped a carton of milk—his midmorning supplement. An interoffice memo stared up at him from his desk. He was to see the director of health services for Chicago National Insurance Company employees at 10:30. It was almost that now.

Gabe left his desk and took the elevator down to the health services department.

"Sit down, Mr. Knapp," the director suggested after they had shaken hands. "We keep files on each of our employees, as you know," he said, reaching for a legal-sized folder beside him.

"There was a time as recent as twenty-five years ago," the man smiled, "when this department operated primarily as a clinic. We dispensed aspirin, bandaged cuts, and took blood pressure. Now that most Americans monitor their own blood pressure we find we can turn our attention to related things."

"Yes," said Gabriel.

"We're missing the report of your recent physical, Mr. Knapp." Gabriel uncrossed, and then recrossed his legs.

"We have made a vigorous search of our files."

"I see," said Gabriel.

"Could it be, Mr. Knapp, that you inadvertently forgot to forward the report to this office?"

"I can check with my secretary," said Gabriel.

"This department," the director explained, "must send quarterly reports on all executives to the board of directors. That report is due at the end of this month. We must have your file complete by then, Mr. Knapp."

Gabriel rose, "I understand," he said.

He climbed the three flights to his office; elevators were difficult to think in. There was no medical report now. He had destroyed it before the rescue mission.

"He's been released," a co-worker offered as the two passed on the stairs.

"Who?" Gabriel called behind him, still ascending.

"That guy they arrested for the Lakeside kidnapping," called the other, descending from view. "He came up with an alibi so they let him go."

Gabriel stopped his climb. How long could he continue to pose, he asked himself. There had been three ungreens in the crowd that afternoon. Who were they? Could they identify him?

And letters were coming again—friendly messages telling of his Adamsville family and friends. His stern parent had written suggesting Gabe spend the next few months as a kind of a rescue expert. The Chicago mission had gone so well, she wrote, Gabriel might consider several more missions. There was word of a birther pregnant in South Bend and due to deliver sometime in February.

How long could this go on? Gabriel resumed his climb. More immediately, he thought finally, he must get through the evening. He had consented to meet Monica's aunt for dinner at Monica's apartment.

"You'll love her," she had predicted. Later she added, laughing, "She's a sociologist, but you'll like her anyway."

When Gabe entered Monica's apartment that evening, the pugent aroma of soybean teriyaki greeted him. Monica offered him a glass of wine.

"No, thanks," he apologized, "just water for now. When's your aunt coming?"

"Pretty soon."

Gabe paced.

"Sit down," Monica suggested. "Don't be nervous."

Gabe positioned himself on the sofa. "Who said I'm nervous?" he protested, smiling.

The doorbell rang. Gabe remained on the sofa; he was not in direct view of the doorway. "Aunt Louise," he heard the pleasure in her voice, "come in! I have a friend here, someone I want you to meet. Here, let me take your coat."

"Monica, Monica," Gabe heard the older woman say, "it's good to be here."

"Come on, I want you to meet someone," her voice came closer.

"Aunt Louise, this is Gabe Knapp. Gabe, this is the aunt I've told you about."

Episode 7

Louise Roanoke and Gabriel Knapp stood facing one another, frozen. Louise Roanoke knew now—with too sudden a force—why the name had sounded familiar. Fragmented thoughts flashed through her brain. Monica dating a green! This man, from the welcoming ceremony at Adamsville, involved with her own niece?

The "rescuer" as a subject of sociological inquiry she had partially grown to understand. Indeed, the emotional and rational need to protect him, a subject, had caused much of her previous consternation over how to answer the Department of the Interior's letter. But that her niece knew and loved the mutant seemed impossible.

Gabriel was suffering himself. He had begun to perspire.

Monica watched the two, confused.

"I'm very glad to make your acquaintance," Dr. Roanoke managed, extending her hand toward Knapp.

Gabriel remembered her face. He had seen the three ungreens at the edge of the crowd that day, watching, taking everything in, soaking it up like sponges. He extended his hand to meet Roanoke's. "I've heard much about you," he stammered. "You're here in Chicago at American University?"

"Yes, right," Louise managed, taking a chair. "Yes. Right."

"Well," attempted Monica, aware of the tension between her guests, "how have your separate paths crossed before now?"

Gabriel eased himself onto the sofa, deliberately not responding to Monica's question. Louise Roanoke held the cards now, he reasoned. He would let her make the first play.

Louise searched Monica's countenance, wondering how much her niece knew about Knapp. "Get us all some wine, why don't you, Monica," she said finally.

Confused and uncomfortable, Monica poured three glasses of wine. Meanwhile Gabe had gone to the kitchen where he refilled his glass of water.

"Still only water, Gabe?" Monica asked.

"Yes, please," he mumbled.

Key concepts:
Cultural relativity
Ethnocentrism
Institutionalization

"That's all right, Monica," the aunt's voice seemed to grow increasingly nervous. "Leave the third glass. One of us can drink it later."

"Aunt Louise," Monica insisted, "what's going on here?"

Dr. Roanoke looked first at her niece and then at Gabriel. She remained silent for a long time. "Gabe," she said at last, "how much have you told my niece about yourself?"

Quickly Monica turned toward Gabriel. "What's going on?" she demanded again.

"I haven't told her everything," Gabe murmured.

Louise helped herself to one of the wine glasses Monica had filled. "Monica," she said, "do you remember when Brad and Connie and I went to Adamsville?"

"Yes, of course," replied the niece.

"Gabe and I saw one another in Adamsville," Roanoke said simply.

"I don't understand," Monica shrugged. Then to Gabe: "Is that true? Were you in Green Colony?"

"Yes," responded Gabriel. "I was in Adamsville."

"Why?"

"I was there on business. I had to go."

"I didn't know Chicago National did business with Green Colony."

"It wasn't that kind of business exactly," Gabe admitted. Then after a pause he added, "Monica, I'm a green."

Monica stared, incredulous.

Gabe had begun to pace. "Could we turn up the lights?" He ran his hand through his hair. "It's awfully dark in here."

Louise flicked a switch on the wall beside her; light flooded the room.

"What kind of business were you doing in Adamsville?" Monica asked slowly. She appeared strangely calm in the immediate shock of Gabe's revelation.

"I had rescued an infant from death," came the simple, direct reply.

"What infant?" Monica asked, her voice rising.

"A baby boy, born where he should never have been born. A green who must be raised in Adamsville by his own people in order to survive. I rescued him, took him home. That's all."

"What are you talking about?" Monica insisted.

"Monica," Louise explained, "when Connie, Brad, and I were in Adamsville, we had occasion to witness a ceremony. It was called a welcoming ceremony. The colony was welcoming an infant into its midst. A member of the community had rescued the infant from death, we were told. The rescued baby had been born outside Adamsville. It was Gabe who rescued the infant."

"I'm sorry," Monica shook her head, "I still don't understand. Where did you get this baby, Gabe?"

Again Gabriel sat down. "Here in Chicago," he said.

"*Where* here in Chicago?" demanded the younger woman.

"Lake Hospital," he said.

"*You* kidnapped that baby?" whispered Monica in disbelief.

"I rescued one of our children," Gabe corrected her.

"You *kidnapped* that baby!" Monica's voice was shrill. "How could you do such a thing?"

"I had to, that's all," Gabriel insisted. "The baby would have died here on the outside. He had to be raised in Adamsville by parents who know how to care for him. I *rescued* him."

"You stole him," Monica breathed. "What about his parents? Did you ever think of his parents?"

"He will have good parents," Gabe replied.

"I'm talking about his *real* parents, Gabriel! What about his mother? Have you read about his mother in the newspapers? She's so grief-stricken she had a nervous breakdown."

"Birthers do not love their children," Gabe replied calmly.

"I don't understand you," Monica shook her head.

"Birthers—people who bear babies—they don't love their infants right away. Parents must grow to love their children."

"That's crazy," Monica turned toward her aunt. "What's going on?"

Louise looked at Gabriel. "Gabe," she said, "why do your people believe that the baby you rescued is a green?"

"He had a green chromosomal father," Gabe answered.

"And his mother was an outsider?"

"Yes."

"Then the baby was only half mutant," Louise said.

"There is no such thing," Gabe flatly replied.

"I don't understand," confessed Dr. Roanoke.

Gabe took a long drink from his water. "There is no such thing as a half-green," he repeated.

"If a baby is born," Dr. Roanoke challenged, "of a green chromosomal father and a nonmutant chromosomal mother, then the baby is a partial mutant."

"A green is a green," Gabe said. "That's all there is to it. There is no such thing as a partial green. A green mutant's genes are always dominant."

"How do you know that?" Roanoke insisted.

"I know it, that's all. It's simply the truth." Gabe was growing angry.

Monica stared into the red wine as it shimmered in her glass. Taking a long, deep breath, she shook her head almost imperceptibly. "I still cannot believe," she said slowly, "that you could do such a thing with no regard whatsoever for the feelings of that infant's real mother."

"The baby's mother," Gabriel reaffirmed wearily, "has no feelings for the child. Birthers do not love their infants."

"You really believe that what you did was right, don't you?" Monica asked, suddenly realizing that what she said was true.

"I'm a moral man. I wouldn't do anything which I considered immoral. Of course the rescue was right." Gabe lowered his voice. "You know, I risked my life to save that baby."

Knapp then explained that he was himself rescued as an infant. "If it had not been for the courage of my own rescuers," he proclaimed, "I would have perished on the outside. I had to do the same for another of my people."

"Is it an Adamsville law that green infants born on the outside must be rescued?" inquired Louise.

"Of course," Gabriel responded.

"Does the law demand that you perform a rescue?" Louise asked.

"No," Gabe said. "Conscience demands that I rescue. The religion I learned from my parents demands that I rescue."

The smell of teriyaki had penetrated Monica's apartment. "Monica," Louise said, aware that the food would soon burn, "are you still interested in serving dinner?"

Monica exchanged her emptied wine glass for the extra one she had poured previously. "I'm not hungry," she whispered.

Louise stood. "Well," she said, straightening her clothes, "you two have plenty to talk about. I think it's best if I go on now."

Monica followed her aunt from the room and, near the front door, helped the older woman with her coat. Louise kissed her niece, then suddenly hugged her. "I'm truly sorry the evening turned out this way," she said.

"I still can't comprehend it," Monica murmured.

● ● ●

It was 10 P.M. when Louise Roanoke left her niece's apartment, and she was tired. But rather than going home, she caught a late ferry to American University Island. For reasons of which she herself was uncertain it had become important to her that she answer Grady's letter immediately. There was no time to confer with her colleagues.

In her office Louise pushed off her shoes, slumped into her comfortably familiar desk chair, and sighed deeply. It all seemed some preposterous nightmare. Monica, her own dear Monica, dating a mutant kidnapper!

Again Dr. Roanoke read the letter she had received from the office of the secretary of the interior. How would she respond now, she wondered. As a sociologist? As a United States citizen who believed in strict law enforcement at least for major crimes of violence? As a fond aunt, concerned and tormented over the involvement of her niece?

Just how much allegiance did she owe the government, Louise asked herself. American University had received substantial federal grants to finance the sociological research of greens. In that sense the government was her employer, was it not? Did she therefore owe the Department of the Interior the whole truth?

What consideration did she owe her subjects, the citizens of Adamsville? The sociologists had gained access to the colony on the premise that what they learned there might help the mutants—not further their chances of annihilation.

What responsibility did Louise have to future nonmutant parents who might unwittingly produce green offspring? Should she not do all within her power to stop any pain these potential victims might suffer?

Finally, how much loyalty did she owe her own niece? Louise had grown close to Monica. Like her aunt, Monica enjoyed batting ideas back and forth. As an attorney she thought deeply about legal and social issues. She believed strongly, for example, that the civil rights of individuals must be vigorously protected. She spoke often of the moral obligation resting upon lawyers, sociologists, and others to protect Americans' inalienable rights. But the women spent only a part of their time together discussing ideas. Even more often they spoke of routine activities, friends and acquaintances. Last week Monica had invited her aunt to meet a "special friend."

Monica had met him, she explained, at a lunch counter one day almost two years ago. Monica had initiated the conversation. "Aren't you eating today?" she had asked the man, noting that in front of him was only a glass of ice water and a cup of coffee.

"Not hungry," he had responded.

"Do you work here in the Loop?" Monica had asked.

"Yes," he said. "You?"

They had talked awhile, Monica told Louise, and then he asked if she would like to go for a walk. Monica agreed and the relationship had begun.

Louise realized that Monica had met many friends since coming to Chicago. Consequently she had suspected the importance of her niece's desire that her aunt become acquainted with this particular man.

"How serious are you about him?" Louise had asked in the straightforward manner their relationship demanded.

"I love him," Monica had replied.

Now Louise Roanoke sat pondering alone in her office. As Monica's aunt she found herself angry that her niece loved a mutant. As a sociologist she chided herself for that anger. Louise reflected: Would she relay to the government Gabriel Knapp's identity, surrendering a person Monica loved to an unsure but dangerous fate?

Dr. Roanoke filled a small pot with cold water and scooped ground coffee into an accompanying metal basket. Soon the aroma of coffee would fill her office.

Then she rolled a sheet of paper into her typewriter. She would rough out her response tonight.

"Two colleagues and I," she wrote, "entered Adamsville, June 28. At that time we witnessed a 'welcoming ceremony,' which marked the acceptance of an infant into the community. It is possible," Louise wrote, "that this infant was 'rescued' without the knowledge of those outsiders caring for the baby at the time.

"As a sociologist I have reason to believe that the 'rescuing' of infants may be behavior that is well institutionalized in Adamsville. It is difficult, however," Roanoke concluded, "to say more without further study."

Louise poured herself a cup of coffee. She wondered what Monica and Gabe were saying to one another.

Episode 8

Monica closed her apartment door behind Louise, then turned to face Gabe. "Listen," she said, taking a long breath, "I made the teriyaki. Do you want some?"

"I'm not hungry," Gabe said. He seated himself on the floor, then reclined so as to place his face directly within the rays of a floor lamp.

"You're a green," Monica said. "Somehow I can't believe this is really happening."

She seated herself on the floor beside him. "Tell me all about yourself," she said.

"Well, I had three parents," Gabriel began, "two men and a woman."

"You mean you had two fathers?"

"I had a chromosomal father," he said slowly, determined, "but he was not my parent."

"You were adopted."

"Monica," he said, "just let me tell you. I was raised in a large home by three parents: two men and one woman. We didn't call them 'mother' or 'father'. We called them 'stern parents' or 'soft parents', according to their personalities."

Monica opened her mouth as if to speak.

"Don't talk," Gabriel urged. "Just listen. My soft parent's name was Jonathan. Jonathan Knapp. He was the oldest of the three nurturing partners, so I received his name.

"My stern parents were Gabriel Jones and Loretta Larson. Gabriel died when I was eleven years old.

"My uncle lived with us for a while. He was Loretta's brother, and he helped with the chores, but he was not part of the contract."

"Who was your real father?"

"Real?" he repeated.

"Who was your chromosomal father?"

"I don't know."

"Don't you care?"

"He was not a chromosomal son of Adam. That much I know. My birther rescued me from him."

"Wouldn't you like to know something about him?"

Gabriel had grown impatient. "Just listen," he said. "I was the only Knapp child. When I was eighteen Loretta and Jonathan severed their nurturing contract."

Key concepts:
Institution of marriage and the family
Kinship
Homogamy

"You mean they got divorced," Monica began to feel she understood.

"No. They had contracted to nurture together until I became eighteen. After that there was no contract, that's all.

"Loyal descendants of Adam contract to nurture with someone of either sex or with two or three people for at least eighteen years. If they accept more children after the first baby, then they remain contracted until the youngest becomes eighteen."

"Do the 'soft parents' and the 'stern parents' have the babies?"

"Perhaps—if they are male and female. In fact, all pure greens are encouraged to increase the race. But sometimes," Gabriel continued, "only males or only females will nurture another couple's baby." He paused. "A woman could birth an infant and then decide not to go into a nurturing contract with anyone. So she would give her baby to a nurturing family."

"Then couples who are not involved in a nurturing contract may conceive children?"

"Yes," Gabe said. "Whatever helps our people to grow in number is morally acceptable."

"What about homosexuality?" Monica asked. "You said just males or just females could enter a nurturing contract. Does that mean they're homosexuals?"

"Not necessarily," Gabe said. "But if they are it doesn't matter so long as they are doing their part either by nurturing or by working at S.T.I.—or in some other way—to help further the cause of greens."

The whole thing had become so implausible to Monica that it had taken on a fictional quality.

"What if nurturing parents want to get divorced before their child is eighteen?" Monica questioned.

"They can't," Gabe explained. "It's against the law."

"Well," she ventured, "if no one gets divorced, then there must be lots of rotten marriages—people no longer in love, just staying together because they have to."

"Parents aren't expected to love one another"—Gabriel was patient—"only to raise green children according to Adam's laws."

"But, Gabe," Monica refilled her glass, "if you and I had a baby and then decided to become nurturing parents to our own baby, wouldn't we love one another?"

Gabriel looked into Monica's eyes. His mind flashed back to a conversation he had had in Adamsville the evening after the rescue. He had gone to a liquidhouse with a fellow mutant named Jacob Lockwood.

Jacob had married on the outside, left his ungreen spouse when the first evidences of his mutation appeared, and only recently returned to Adamsville.

"Do you miss her?" Gabe had asked his friend, thinking of his own relationship with Monica.

"Not anymore," Jacob had replied, toying with the plastic straw in his drink.

"Did you love her?"

"They talk about love all the time on the outside," Jacob said, "but they can't tell you exactly what it is. We don't talk about love here, you know that."

"Why did you marry her, Jacob?" Gabe had persisted.

"I thought I loved her." Jacob motioned the bartender for another drink. "But all greens know that love between adults doesn't last."

"I know they taught that in school, and my parents always said that. And religion teaches it too. But..." Gabe's voice had trailed off.

"You've been outside too long," Jacob had observed. "Come home where you belong before they ruin you."

Now Gabriel pressed his palm against the crown of his head. "If you and I," he said, studying Monica's face, "were to enter a nurturing contract, we would love one another." He paused. "Monica," he said resolutely, "I do love you."

The woman shifted, "Before, when we talked about marriage," she said, "you didn't mention your being a mutant."

Gabriel sat quietly, not answering.

"Gabe," Monica continued, "last June, when you told me you had to leave the city on business for Chicago National, you lied to me."

"I'm sorry," he said. "You wouldn't have understood."

"Well, I have to agree with you there," she spurted, rising from her place on the floor and entering the kitchen where she turned off the heating surface under the teriyaki.

Returning to the living room, she asked, growing angry, "How many babies have you rescued, Gabriel?"

"Only one."

"Only the one from Lake Hospital in June? You never kidnapped any children before this?"

"No." He placed his hands upon Monica's shoulders and peered into her eyes. "You probably won't believe me, but I didn't want to do this one. I was pressured into it."

"But you thought it was right!"

Knapp shrugged, raising his arms in the air. "Yes, I think it was the right thing to do: saving an infant's life. I didn't do it before now because I'm a coward, I guess. I began to like it here in Chicago. For a while I forgot who I was. Besides," he added, "I was afraid I'd get caught."

The two remained silent for a while.

"What would your people do," Monica questioned finally, "if you were caught?"

"If they considered me a loyal Adamsville citizen they would help me however they could. But I have been disloyal, and so I don't know."

"How have you been disloyal?"

"I've disappointed my parents," Gabe said. "Jonathan Knapp, my soft parent, is ill now. I visited him after the rescue. He had expected me to return to Adamsville for good before my thirtieth birthday."

"Why?"

"It's one of Adam's laws."

"Wasn't Jonathan pleased that you had performed a rescue?"

"Yes, of course," Gabriel admitted. "But now he misses me."

"And what about your other living parent, Loretta?"

"She wants me to perform more rescues. She feels that I must redeem myself for my previous lack of commitment to the community —and for my lack of appreciation."

"Lack of appreciation for what exactly?"

"First of all for my own rescue. And then, of course, for the family life I enjoyed with her and Jonathan and Gabriel."

"Do you feel bad that Jonathan misses you?" Monica asked, unsure whether she would ever understand this man.

"Well, of course I do." Gabriel's voice sounded hurt.

"Then why didn't you stay in Adamsville with him last June?"

Gabe Knapp inhaled a long, deep breath. He rubbed his fingers over his forehead, then exhaled. "I wanted to come back," he said quietly, "to my job and to you."

Monica left her chair, resuming her former place on the floor near Gabriel. "Gabe," she said after a long pause, "did you really think we could be married?"

"I don't know," he answered then. "I think so. Some of our people have married ungreens." "Then it's permissible in Adamsville to marry someone from outside the colony?" Monica was surprised.

"It is discouraged now," Gabe replied, "especially by some members who feel we should separate ourselves completely from ungreens. But before there were so many of us, posing greens married outsiders often."

"And what happened once these posers turned green?"

"They went home."

Monica's features hardened. "They simply left their mates and returned to the colony, is that right?"

"Yes," Gabriel admitted. "No outsider has ever lived in Adamsville."

Monica stood. "And what, Gabriel, if these mixed couples had borne children? Did your green people kidnap their own mates' children?"

Gabe didn't answer. Against his skull the word "rescue," like a hammer, pounded over and over. "Rescue, Monica," he wanted to scream at the top of his lungs. Not "kidnap" or "steal," but "rescue." He studied the angry pain upon the woman's face. "Maybe," he said at last, "you would have wanted to come with me to Adamsville." He knew even as he heard himself say it that this had always been a frivolous, irresponsible dream. Monica could never have been comfortable in Adamsville. Gabe was not even sure she would have been allowed entry. He lit a cigarette.

"Anyway," he said, drawing the smoke deep into his lungs, "I had begun to think that maybe I wasn't really a mutant, that maybe my skin would never turn green, that perhaps I was rescued by mistake. In that case I would never have had to return to Adamsville. We could have been married and lived normally, here on the outside."

This new information confused Monica still further, momentarily diminishing her anger. "Why did you think you might not be a green?"

"When I was twenty-five or so, my skin didn't begin to turn. With every succeeding year that I didn't mature physically, I nursed the thought more and more that I was not really a mutant. Then I was thirty and still my skin hadn't greened. My parents had taught me that virtually all greens mature before their thirtieth birthday."

"But you're convinced now that you definitely are a green, that you were not rescued by mistake?"

"Yes," he said, extinguishing the cigarette, "I know now for certain that I'm green. That's largely why I decided to perform the rescue."

"Why are you certain now that you are a green?" Monica asked.

"I had a physical," he said. "The mutation showed up. I almost told you several times." He lowered his voice. "I'm really very sorry."

They sat quietly for some time. Gabe smoked a second cigarette.

It was Monica who broke the long silence. "This is why you seldom drink anything but water, why you eat so little," she said more to herself than to Gabe. Relentlessly the reality of the evening enveloped her.

"Monica," Gabe said apologetically, "perhaps we both need time to think all this over."

She nodded, sighing deeply. "I don't think we should see one another—at least for a while," she said.

Episode 9

It was mid-March, 2027. Gabe sat alone on the terrace of his apartment. His sleeves rolled up and his shirt unbuttoned, he leaned back in his lounge and closed his eyes. It was early evening. The sun shone reasonably warm for the first time in months. "Relax," he thought as energy penetrated his being. "Nourish yourself."

He was troubled. A news leak from the United States district attorney's office had recently disclosed that mutants were indeed suspected of the many unsolved kidnappings which had occurred over the preceding years. Still, Gabe realized, only Monica, Batterson, Duncan, and Roanoke knew either of his mutation or of his personal involvement in the Lake Hospital mission. While he had not spoken with Monica—except briefly when their paths crossed accidentally—they had remained politely friendly. He was reasonably certain that she would not go to the authorities with information condemning him.

Constance Batterson had visited Gabriel in January, explaining that she and her colleagues considered responsibility to their subjects a matter of vital importance. The sociologists would not disclose Knapp's name. Moreover, they would refuse to testify in court should Gabe ultimately be arrested and tried.

No other outsider, Gabe repeatedly reminded himself, suspected him. He had left no evidence, no fingerprints, nothing anyone would be able to trace.

Yet he was tormented. Since the news leak had appeared on front pages throughout the nation, violence had erupted along Adamsville borders. Gangs armed with guns, knives, clubs, and rocks harassed Adamsville guards. APIK grew daily in strength, demanding extermination of what the group now openly called "green monsters." Several other groups, each for different reasons, condemned the chlorophyllics.

The day before, a young man in Seattle had been torn from his automobile as he drove home from work and fatally beaten. A group of hostile nonmutants had thought him a poser. Gabriel knew that he was not. The growing violence disturbed him. "You're alone out here," he told himself. "Soon you'll have to go home."

But he persisted in his refusal to return. He was thirty-three now.

54

Key concepts:
Institution of religion
Ritual
Institution of education
Institutional integration

While it had been nearly a year since the compulsory physical examination had convinced him that any doubts about his being a mutant were unfounded, his skin continued in its refusal to change.

Gabriel knew there was only one cause for the failure of a green's flesh to mature: disloyalty. And a disloyal green would forever be distrusted. He would go home to disgrace.

Resolved to "take one day at a time," Gabriel Knapp had managed so far to keep his position at Chicago National. The medical file in the department of health services had never been completed. The report had gone—several times now—to the board of directors lacking information on Knapp. Every three months Gabe received the same memo: "Please respond re your medical examination. We have no record of such in this office." Every three months, Gabriel folded the memo, took it home, and burned it.

Knapp watched the March evening sun descend. He rose and entered his apartment, pulling the sliding door shut behind him. Not sufficiently refreshed, he poured himself a glass of milk, the supplement he continued to require. Never, he chided himself as he swallowed, had he been able to do without it.

The door bell rang. When he opened a tiny aperture through which he might view his unexpected visitor, he stepped back in amazement.

The bell rang again. Gabe opened the door. "What are you doing here?" he blurted. And then, giving his guest no time to answer, "Were you followed?"

"Of course not," replied a young man in his early twenties. "Hurry and let me in, will you? I'm nervous as hell on the outside now."

The visitor shoved past Gabriel into the apartment. "It wasn't my idea to come," he said, removing his jacket. "I'm doing this for Jacob Lockwood. You and he used to be pretty good friends, he said, back

55

in school. You snuck off and ran into some chocolate candy trouble together or something. Anyway, he's still fond of you. He persuaded me to come."

Bewildered, Gabriel ushered his guest into the living room. "Is it bright enough in here for you, Daniel? We can go into the bedroom if you like. I had some fluorescent tubes installed—"

"It's fine here, Gabriel," the younger, not-yet-matured green interrupted.

Gabe eased himself into a chair, sliding a partially full cigarette package into a drawer in the table beside him. Green religion prohibited smoking. To burn tobacco leaves was considered a symbolic infraction against "the photosynthetic universe."

"How's Jonathan?" Gabriel asked, unclear about the cause of this unprecedented visit.

"Dead," came Daniel Adamson's cold, succinct response.

Gabriel's jaw dropped. "That's impossible," he murmured.

"Greens die just like nonmutants, you know," Dan said sarcastically.

"Is that why you came here—to tell me?"

"No, Gabriel. Jonathan died several months ago. He lay in the sun on his burial bed without you."

During the religious funeral rite, Adamsville relatives placed the stripped body of the deceased upon a sacred burial bed. The burial bed consists of a rock slab, 6 feet by 3 feet, over which a thick layer of green leaves has been carefully placed. Mourners keep vigil while the body lies in the sun. Once the blanket of leaves become parched, the deceased is buried, naked, with no casket of any kind.

The news of Jonathan's death had made Gabe feel weak. "Listen," he said, embarrassed, "I was just pouring a glass of supplement. Excuse me while I get it." Dizzy, he rose and went into the kitchen.

When he returned, Daniel asked, "Still taking supplement? You're too old for that, aren't you?"

"I can't help it," Gabe confessed. Shock and grief had undermined Gabriel's usual resolve to hide the weakness.

"Adam's law teaches that no green use supplement unless it is absolutely necessary," Dan preached.

"I know that," Gabe replied with impatience. "I went to school too. I learned religion just as you did. I get weak, that's all. Forget it."

"Jacob thought," Daniel ventured, realizing that he had offended his host, "that maybe by the Lake Hospital rescue you had proven yourself. He hopes you will soon begin to turn. He wanted me to encourage you to come home for the ceremony. The vernal equinox isn't far off, you know."

THE STORY OF ADAMSVILLE

Adam Jones III had been a religious prophet. It was his law that all greens must mature.

Maturation rites occurred twice yearly on the occasions of the vernal and autumnal equinoxes. "Henceforth," Adam Jones III had written, "my progeny shall gather at the time when the sun crosses the equator making night and day all over the earth of equal length: that is, at the time of the vernal and autumnal equinoxes, occurring approximately March 21 and September 22. During the equinoxes, symbols of God's love and guidance, my people shall, by celebrating the onset of full greenness among their young, reaffirm their faith in God's plan."

God's plan, Gabriel and his peers had learned in school, at home, and during religious rituals, depended upon Adamsville for execution. Adam, prophet sent from God, had helped to father a new people.

The semiannual maturing ceremony had, since Adam Jones originated it, developed into an extravagant affair. During predawn hours on the morning of the equinox, the colony gathered in the park adjacent to Elderhome. It was sacred ground: To set foot in the park was to pray. As the sun rose, greens chanted thanks for the eternal source of energy, God's ultimate gift.

At noon when the sun reached the center of the sky, those who were to mature advanced to the sacred platform upon which Gabe Knapp had presented the rescued baby. The platform, draped in green velvet and flanked with cactus and desert flowers, had been decorated by Adamsville children.

Green velvet cloaks draped the candidates for maturity as they walked in procession toward the platform. A band played while they, one by one, removed their garments, letting them fall from their shoulders until they stood naked before their fellows. As those maturing gleamed green in the sunshine, Ruth and Michael Jones led the crowd in a religious chant.

"We are the future people of earth," Ruth called.

"We are the culmination of God's evolutionary plan," Michael chanted.

Later matured mutants advanced into the Great Hall, some for the first time.

All greens, Adam had written, must mature. It was later ruled, however, that if their skin did not become bright green by the time of their twenty-eighth birthday, greens must—after public repentance for their apparent sins of disloyalty—participate in the maturing ceremony.

"Outsiders have attacked our guards," Gabriel's guest had been explaining. "Gangs converge upon our gates, shouting insults, threatening murder. They may thwart God's plan."

"Now," Daniel continued, "our people are becoming separated from one another, joining factions. Larry Jones claims that Elders are no longer capable of ruling, that they sin in their lack of commitment."

"Why?"

"They allowed three outsiders into the colony," Dan said flatly. "Larry feels that our troubles stem from that time."

"I agree," Gabriel said. "How do you think I felt, standing there chanting before our people, when I looked out into the throng and saw three ungreens? I am the one who could suffer most from this."

"The Elders," Daniel said, "thought you intended to remain in Adamsville. You were thirty-two years old, Gabriel! When you consented to perform the rescue, the Elders assumed you had chosen to repent and were returning for good."

Gabriel said nothing. The thought of a public confession sickened him.

"When you left again," Daniel continued, "it was apparent the Elders had misjudged you. Larry claims they sin by occasionally ignoring light-break. Hence, even their secular judgments are no longer valid."

Light-break, while of much lesser religious importance than either the maturing or the welcoming ceremonies, was a mandatory worship service. As greens lay on the park grounds or in their glass-roofed homes, absorbing solar energy, they became not only physically but spiritually stronger.

Daniel continued speaking. "And Larry says Duncan must go."

"Duncan is still there then?" Gabe was surprised.

"Yes. He's been there eight months now."

Gabriel rubbed his chin. "Why did Jacob send you here?" he asked after a pause.

"He wants you to come home. He believes that you have sinned. Your transgression must be confessed and forgiven before we will again be blessed with peace."

"So," Gabriel said, "*my* sin has helped cause this turmoil? What about the sins of the Elders?"

"Larry is not strong enough yet to defrock the Elders. But he wants *all* sin rooted from the community. And your sin is grievous."

Gabriel Knapp stood. "Tell them all," he said, "to tackle their most crucial problem. It is the Elders who have sinned! I admit that I have doubted. But my transgression is nothing compared to theirs!" Gabriel paused. "When Larry has accomplished the eviction of the outsider, Duncan, I will begin to consider coming home."

The visitor changed his expression. "Gabe," he said hesitantly, "don't you feel guilty for your transgressions against God and Adam?"

Gabriel thought a long time. "Daniel," he said, "when I left Adamsville for college, I took some courses in genetics."

Daniel listened, uncertain of the relevance of this.

"I learned that some genes are either dominant or recessive, like the ones which determine eye color, for instance. If a person with blue eyes and a person with brown eyes conceive a child, the child's eyes will be blue—not bluish brown."

"I know that," Dan responded impatiently.

Gabe persisted. "But sometimes genes don't work that way. If a white outsider and a black outsider conceive a child, that child will be neither white nor black but a mixture of the two."

Dan gazed at Gabriel.

"Our religion teaches," Gabe spoke slowly, "that a green's genes are always dominant."

"Of course."

"But that religious tenet has not been subjected to scientific verification."

Dan grinned sarcastically. "And do you propose testing religious doctrines in a scientific laboratory?" he smirked.

Gabriel Knapp stared at the younger mutant intensely. "Our religion teaches," he continued, "that I drink supplements and that my skin does not mature because I have somehow been disloyal."

"Do you deny that?"

"I don't deny that I have had doubts. But there is a second possibility, Daniel."

"And what is that?"

"That mutant genes are not always dominant. That I was born of a chromosomal father who had dark skin, and I have inherited that complexion. The inherited darkness of my flesh may conceal the chlorophyll in it. And it is possible that, because I had only one green chromosomal parent, I do not photosynthesize to the extent that you do and that is why I continue to rely on supplement."

Dan stared in surprise. "You are a heretic," he whispered. "You have demonstrated here—right now—a degree of disloyalty that I have never witnessed before! It's no wonder that your skin remains dull."

"I rescued," Gabriel reminded his visitor firmly.

"And I find it difficult to understand why," Dan replied with sarcasm.

"Because my religion—while I often doubt it—is still very much part of me. When criticized by outsiders"—Gabe recalled his final evening with Monica—"I find myself defending our religious beliefs and practices vehemently."

"Larry is right," Dan said. "He wants Adamsville to establish its own university. He believes we must stop sending our young people away to schools where they can be taught heresy and untruth by outsiders."

Later Daniel explained that he had to leave. He was to catch a plane back to Phoenix that night.

When he departed, a woman of sixty, parked on the street outside, reached across the front seat of her dark-colored vehicle to a portable telephone. Drawing it to her lips, she said: "FBI Agent Garcia reporting. Green suspect presently departing Shore Towers apartments. Proceeding north on foot. . ."

Since his departure from Adamsville Daniel had been followed.

Episode 10

Restless and disorderly demonstrations plagued the second National Conference on Human Mutations when it opened May 10, 2027, in Washington, D.C. Divergent groups pressed unsuccessfully for admission into the auditorium where scientists who had assembled the previous year would again discuss—and attempt to define—greens.

SPHR (Society for the Protection of the Human Race) had rented three floors in a hotel adjacent to the symposium headquarters. Espousing the necessity for "human purity," SPHR vigorously opposed assimilation of "evolutionary throwbacks."

Representatives of APIK (Association for the Prevention of Infant Kidnappings) emerged to promote what they called "preventive justice." Eagerly they urged arrest and prosecution of "all green posers discovered in normal society."

Members of Concerned Citizens for National Defense (CCND) milled about, cornering scientists and distributing literature. The United States must attack Green Colony immediately, they convincingly insisted, in order to thwart an internal military threat to the government.

Still other groups demonstrated in opposition to these factions. Civil Liberty for All (CLA), an organization committed to the legal defense and protection of mutants, was recognizable by green armbands worn by its members. Representatives of the National Farmers Organization were in Washington urging gradual and "orderly" integration of greens. The food growers had grown dependent upon solar transistors. To destroy Green Colony and S.T.I., they argued, would be to destroy the world's hope for survival.

SVP (Stop Violence to Posers), a coalition of influential American businessmen, joined in the plea for harmony. It had become impossible, they noted, to contact S.T.I. sales representatives. Decreasing access to solar transistors would throw United States industry deeper into economic depression.

As Bradley Duncan labored past the noisy commotion into the conference hall where he would be principal speaker, he remarked to himself on the excess of uniformed policemen. The situation on the

Key concepts:
Institution of politics
Institution of economics
Institutional integration

---

outside, he realized with full force, had grown critical during the period of his participant observation in Adamsville.

Upon entering the hall Brad spotted his colleages. They stood casually near a large coffee maker at the rear of the auditorium.

"Morning," he said, approaching. He helped himself to a complimentary donut from a tray near the coffee. "Sure is nice," he chuckled, "to see food displayed like this out in public again. I was beginning to feel like some kind of pervert, sneaking quick meals, always eating in solitude."

Adamsville's Elders had granted Duncan use of an unoccupied glass residence near Sunlight Liquidhouse. Twice monthly Brad had driven into Phoenix for food and supplies.

"We hear you downed a lot of protein capsules," Constance Batterson smiled.

"And how did you survive without your beer?" Louise Roanoke laughed.

Duncan had left Adamsville just three days before. He had not yet had a long visit with his friends.

Several other conference members gathered, introducing themselves and shaking Brad's hand. "You've become something of a celebrity," Batterson teased, whispering into Brad's ear. "I hope your speech is good!"

A gavel sounded from the front of the room. Fifteen minutes later Duncan approached the podium.

"Fellow scientists," he began. "I am speaking to you today because, as a sociologist, I spent almost ten months as an Adamsville resident. When I left there just the other day," Brad announced with regret, "several Adamsville residents and I decided that it would be in their best interest if I did not return."

Duncan shifted. A ripple ran through the audience.

"During my stay there, however, I gained some understanding of green culture. It is my hope that I can share a bit of that understanding with you."

Roanoke and Batterson sat near the front of the lecture hall. Louise smiled encouragingly toward Brad. Her mind went back to her own address the previous year. So much had changed. Louise had spent months of painful soul-searching since she first met and recognized Gabriel Knapp. Her decision to relay to the secretary of interior information regarding greens' belief in rescuing, and the subsequent leak of the information to the news media, had promoted national turmoil. Louise would always feel partially responsible for the violence that followed.

While Constance Batterson had expressed sympathy throughout Louise's personal misery, the younger sociologist remained convinced that her colleague should not have sent the letter. Sociological truth, Connie maintained, could only be ascertained through vigorous refusal to cooperate with the established and powerful forces in society. In an inevitable conflict between humanity's powerful and powerless, a sociologist, Batterson believed, was morally bound not to strengthen the might of the powerful. Louise had erred, Connie had suggested, realizing even while she did that many sociologists—after considering the moral issue seriously—would have proceeded exactly as had her friend and colleague.

But Louise had suffered over something else too. She knew that Gabe's involvement in a kidnapping had shocked and hurt her niece. "He should have told Monica about the mutation early in their relationship," Louise had complained to Connie during a discussion they'd had the previous November.

"Agreed," Connie had said. "And then what?"

"And then Monica could have broken it off long before the two became so involved," Louise had responded.

"What's this?" Connie had smirked, attempting in vain to cheer her friend. "An Ode to Homogamy?"

"Monica couldn't survive in Adamsville," Louise had said then. "She'd die of malnutrition! And Gabe wouldn't be comfortable out here." She paused. "That kidnapping was an awful thing," she murmured.

It had been several seconds before Connie spoke. "What about the concept of cultural relativity?" she ventured.

"Cultural relativity is necessary as a methodological attitude," Roanoke had replied. "It need not be a general moral conviction."

"And I thought sociologists tended to be liberal thinkers," Connie had chuckled.

"And do middle-aged aunts?" Louise had retorted.

Roanoke's attention returned to Duncan.

"Elders Ruth and Michael Jones," Duncan was saying, "have, since Adam's death, made virtually all the community's decisions. They assign community-owned land and housing to residents and exercise final authority over citizens' occupations. Adamsville's Elders are both political and religious rulers. The children of a prophet, it is reasoned, are inclined to neither sacred nor secular error. Until recently it had been assumed that Ruth and Michael would rule until their deaths.

"Changes are occurring now, however. Primarily they are the result of the charismatic personality and organizational ability of a younger mutant named Larry Jones.

"Larry Jones is a fully matured green of forty-four whose epidermis dazzles. This physical trait, I have observed, contributes to his leadership ability. Adamsville residents trust their greenest members most.

"Larry Jones is a great grandson of Adam Jones III. Larry's grandfather, David, had—before he was murdered—married a nonmutant and fathered three children. One of these offspring, a female, eventually married her first cousin, the son of Adam Jones's daughter Ann. Larry Jones was born of this union." Duncan swallowed from a glass of water which had been placed near the podium. "I burden you with this genealogical information," he continued, wiping his lips with the back of his hand, "to demonstrate that Larry Jones is—as are all mutants—the descendant of both greens and ungreens. The fact that his skin—and that of others like him—is extremely bright supports a religious doctrine in Adamsville, namely, that the color of a chlorophyllic's skin is not dependent upon chromosomal genealogy, but upon religious conviction. The more secular tenet corresponding to that religious dogma has become something of a maxim in Adamsville. 'A green is a green', the saying goes. 'A green's chromosomes are always dominant'."

Duncan paused. "Larry's luminance, then, attests to his religious loyalty. Since secular allegiance cannot be separated from religious devotion, it has long been assumed that Larry would advance to leadership upon the deaths of Ruth and Michael.

"To understand the reasons for this widespread social agreement, it is helpful first to know something about economics in Adamsville.

"Solar Transistors, Inc., began with a federal grant issued by ERDA in 2004. It was Larry Jones, then an inexperienced youth of twenty-one, who successfully convinced the federal government of his family's scientific potential.

"This fact remains much appreciated among Adamsvillers. Members of the community are aware that, as a result of their unique physiological circumstances, they face what could be a serious economic difficulty. That is, the older and more experienced members of the community have matured; the greenness of their skin forces them to remain upon family territory. As public relations ambassadors or S.T.I. sales personnel they are useless.

"The two dozen sales representatives who had until recently called upon businesses throughout the United States were all posers under twenty-five years old. It falls upon the immature and less experienced members of the colony, then, to contact prospective consumers. Often immatured greens find themselves unequal to the challenge. Larry Jones did not.

"His reward was a position as the third member of the board of directors of S.T.I. He controls 40 percent of the corporation's stock. Ruth and Michael own over 50 percent of the S.T.I. shares. That S.T.I. now manufactures solar weapons for the military defense of Adamsville attests to the influence and power of board member Larry Jones.

"The physical facilities of Solar Transistors, Inc., include several expansive, single-story buildings on the outskirts of the small city at the center of the family's property. The single most important resource to their product—solar energy—appears limitless and is considered by Adamsvillers a gift from God.

"A second necessary resource, labor, is supplied by the mutants themselves. While highly automated, the plant employs several hundred workers, all matured greens who must remain upon the property.

"Adamsville does need to purchase some materials to produce transistors. S.T.I. has obtained these from Japan. Larry, after acquiring the ERDA money, spent several months in Japan. While sources there have continued to supply Adamsville by mail, greens believe strongly that Larry's initial contact with Japanese industrialists was vitally necessary."

Dr. Duncan took another long drink of water, then continued. "I mentioned earlier," he said, "that things had begun to change in Adamsville. The once harmonious community is rocked with political rumblings. Larry Jones, charismatic and luminous, leads a faction of greens that I have come to call 'radical militarists'. They are dedicated to complete separation of greens from the outside. Larry often reminds fellow mutants that his grandfather was murdered by ungreens. But perhaps more important are the economic bases for dissension.

"Larry's goal, it appears now, is to diversify Adamsville's industrial base. He feels that the colony must manufacture goods and services that might be consumed by greens themselves—and on a large scale. As a result the colony's economy should ultimately become independent of outsiders. Then, Larry and his followers reason, Adamsville would be in the position to refuse solar transistors to outside customers at will. And with that economic hammer, radical militarists foresee the advent of national and international political power."

Duncan stopped momentarily, allowing his message to sink in. He proceeded: "The Elders, on the other hand, are convinced that Adamsville should work with ungreens. Their followers remind their fellows of the community's need to continue economic relations with ungreens in Japan, for example. Cooperationists argue that political power rests in the potential to manufacture as many solar transistors as possible. This potential must not be lessened by diversification within S.T.I. Adamsville does not yet have sufficient labor power, they contend, to diversify.

"Cooperationists argue further that only when Adamsville promotes communication with the outside will ungreens begin to understand mutants. And subsequent to that understanding matured greens might one day leave Adamsville, taking influential positions with outside-owned corporations, gaining access to policy-making positions within local and federal government, and consequently advancing the green cause."

Duncan shuffled his papers. He had talked a long time. It was almost noon when he finished. The majority of attending scientists were surprised, therefore, when the chair announced that it would consider one further motion before adjournment.

From the rear of the hall a middle-aged conference member advanced to the podium. She placed a single sheet of paper before her and read. "Be it resolved," she began in a clear, strong voice, "that this body of scientists, representing the accumulated knowledge of humanity, has determined green mutants to be harmful evolutionary throwbacks, pre-human beings, whose continued existence threatens humanity as we know it." Someone seconded the motion.

Batterson, Roanoke, and Duncan—along with others—were stunned. Louise Roanoke stood.

"This is impossible!" she exclaimed. "We don't have all the facts. How can we as scientists make a judgment without sufficient data? If we vote yes on this resolution we are of no more academic credibility than the groups outside struggling for the victory of their own economic, political, and social interests. If we concur with this resolution, fellow conference members, we do not deserve to be called scientists."

A long and heated debate carried into the afternoon. Several hours later the exhausted and hungry scholars tabled the resolution for one year. They did so by the small margin of five votes.

Episode 11

On May 16, 2027, a two-month-old infant was kidnapped from a collapsible stroller at Kennedy Airport in New York City. Two days later a gang of nonmutants converged upon a campsite near Tucson, Arizona. It had been rumored that a young woman and the kidnapped baby were resting there. In the ensuing violence both the woman and baby were fatally shot. Subsequent identification procedures confirmed that the younger victim was indeed the infant who had been seized in New York. An autopsy of the woman accompanying the child revealed "chlorophyll capable of photosynthesis within the epidermis."

May 25, 2027, United States Senator Malcolm Adams, Democrat from Florida, introduced a bill that would officially deny mutants the right to vote in federal elections until their status had been specifically defined as human. The bill would cause bitter and lengthy debate.

On June 5 three unidentified persons drove from Flagstaff, Arizona, to Adamsville where they attacked and murdered one of two chlorophyllic guards. The surviving mutant fired a laser into the escaping auto, killing one of the three and seriously wounding another.

June 10, 2027, the Arizona State Legislature passed two bills. The first, LB 431, demanded that individuals undergo thorough physical examinations—including biochemical tests—before receiving marriage licenses. The second, LB 432, prohibited marriage between mutants and nonmutants.

On June 15, 2027, FBI Agent K. Jeffers phoned the president of Chicago National Insurance Company. Company employee Gabriel Knapp, he explained, had been visited in his apartment at Lake Shore Towers March 14, 2027, at approximately 6 P.M. by a male in his early twenties. The visitor had been followed from Green Colony, Jeffers related, and was known to have returned there. Jeffers requested that

Key concepts:
Stratification
Caste system vs. class system

Chicago National forward available information on Gabriel Knapp to the Federal Bureau of Investigation.

June 17 the director of health services for Chicago National received a memo from the company's president. The memo requested that the file on employee Gabriel Knapp be completed immediately.

That afternoon someone from the health services department contacted the physician who had examined Gabe. Three days later the physician mailed the insurance company the following communication:

"As you know, the doctor-patient relationship demands absolute privacy. Abiding by that professional standard, I have until now offered no one other than Mr. Knapp information concerning his medical examination one year ago.

"It has become less apparent, however, that this individual falls into that category of patients concerning whom a physician is morally and legally bound to secrecy. Therefore, I am enclosing a copy of Mr. Knapp's medical report, compiled last June, 2026."

○ ○ ○

On June 24, 2027, at approximately 11 A.M. Gabriel's secretary buzzed him on the interoffice communication system. "Mr. Knapp," he said, "the vice president in charge of personnel would like to see you in his office at one o'clock this afternoon."

"Thank you," Gabriel responded mechanically.

Half an hour later Gabe opened his drawer and took out the loaded handgun he had purchased several weeks before. Slipping it into his pocket—as he automatically did now whenever leaving the privacy of either his office or apartment—he rose to exit the office.

At the door he glanced backward into the room that had become a symbol of his success and consequently a source of pride. "Plush place," he remarked to himself, shaking his head. "Damn plush place," he repeated, this time with bitterness, then left the office.

He walked toward the lake as he had done so many times before. The sun felt good against his shoulders; the breeze was warm. His thoughts turned to Monica. He missed her. He had heard through rumor that she had joined Civil Liberty for All. After hearing that, Gabe had begun to hope that she would contact him.

He had reasoned that Monica's enlisting in CLA might mean that she would consider seeing him again. But she hadn't phoned. Gabe had been forced to conclude that the woman's membership in CLA was a result of her conviction that in the United States all intelligent beings deserved equal representation under the law. Nothing more.

Gabe had avoided making new friends, growing increasingly isolated over the past ten months. Of the three sociologists whom he had seen in the crowd the day of the rescue, it was Constance Batterson with whom he had lately kept closest contact. She had visited his apartment several times. Occasionally Gabe had gone to her office at American University.

"I have so many questions to ask you," Dr. Batterson had grinned. "How many in-depth interviews do you think you can bear?"

"As many as you like," Gabe had replied, figuring the forthcoming discussions might lessen his loneliness.

Dr. Batterson, along with a team of graduate students, had begun to compile results on a questionnaire she had mailed some months before. The research would yield data concerning the extent of and reasons for ungreens' animosity toward greens. Gabriel's understanding of green culture, Constance had explained, would help her interpret this raw data with greater preception.

Batterson and Knapp found themselves talking for hours at a time. "Why do you think ungreens are opposed to greens' gaining status or power in broader society?" Constance asked often. "Is it because those who do have power refuse to share it and consequently deny greens access to that power? Or is it because green religion really does deny some of the basic moral principles upon which our culture is based?"

Once when Constance had asked this, Gabe had thought awhile, then said, "What moral principles does my religion deny?"

"You felt conscience-bound to rescue," Connie offered. "Kidnapping is opposed to our moral code." Batterson meditated a moment. Later she had said, "Maybe it's good for the larger society to deny power to people who would kidnap infants without discretion."

"Maybe," Gabriel had debated, "but it is not good for *green* people to have to sneak around, hiding their mutations, hurrying home to safety once their skin begins to mature. If we knew our children could survive on the outside even after their skin began to change color, there would be no rescue."

"What would green children need in order to survive on the outside?"

Gabe's response was direct. "Respect," he said.

The discussions continued over several months. "What status will you have in Adamsville if and when you return there?" Batterson had asked once.

"Very low," Gabe had replied. "I will be assigned a home in the valley with other dull greens. I won't be allowed to work in any decision-making positions at S.T.I. I won't be able to enter Elderhome. I can join a nurturing contract, but not to raise offspring of pure greens."

"Why?" Connie had questioned.

"Because I lack sufficient allegiance," Gabe had answered straightforwardly. "Therefore I would be considered dangerous in decision-making positions. I would be a scandal in positions of prestige."

"Then your society believes it is functional to deny dull greens equal rights and opportunities?" Dr. Batterson probed.

"Yes."

"But you have a well-educated economic mind and several years' experience with a major insurance company," Batterson pointed out.

"Still," Gabe had replied, "greens with dull skin often do make mistakes. Besides," he added, "many dull greens seem to be really quite lazy. It is as if they were ill."

Often lethargic, dulls moved more slowly than did their counterparts. Prone to dizzy spells, they often found it difficult to complete a regular day's work without either rest or—more often—supplement.

"I see," Connie had responded. "And are they satisfied with their rank?"

"They know that they have been disloyal and so they accept their position."

Gabe recalled parts of these discussions now as he walked near Lake Michigan. He would miss these conversations with Dr. Batterson when he eventually left Chicago for good.

Gabe didn't return to his office until shortly before his one o'clock appointment. Seated at his desk, he drank a cup of coffee and smoked a cigarette. He had forced himself not to think about the forthcoming meeting. When he had smoked a second cigarette, he ground it into an ashtray and proceeded to the executive suite of the vice president in charge of personnel.

"Sit down, Mr. Knapp," the vice president began courteously.

Gabriel sat down.

"I have received information from your examining physician." He looked at Gabe. "You're a green," he said.

Gabe stared into the other man's eyes. "Yes," he said.

"The FBI contacted us several days ago. They wanted your complete file. We cooperated."

The file, Knapp realized, would contain Gabriel's requests to take sick days. A little checking would reveal that Gabriel Knapp had been absent from work June 28, 2026. He was no longer safe on the outside.

"Mr. Knapp," the executive continued, "your work for us has been exemplary. We hate to lose you. But," he paused briefly, "we know that greens make a practice of returning to Green Colony at just about the time they have become most valuable to their employers. Chicago National has already spent a lot of money training you. We have learned to count on you. We don't want to become even more dependent upon your talents and skills only to have you leave us at what might be a critical time."

"We would not leave, sir, if people with green skin could live safely and with respect on the outside."

"Mr. Knapp," the vice president said firmly, "we will have to let you go. I'm sorry."

Gabriel stood and extended his hand. His superior did likewise. "You may finish the week if you like," he said.

Gabriel returned to his own office. He opened his briefcase and emptied into it some personal belongings from his desk drawers. He took a picture of Monica from the top of his desk. Half an hour later, saying nothing to his secretary, he left Chicago National.

He walked to Illinois State Bank where he withdrew the balances from both his savings and his checking accounts.

Later at his apartment he wrote a letter to his landlord explaining that he had been transferred and must vacate the apartment before the termination of his lease.

From his bedroom closet he pulled three suitcases. He would take what he could. He packed cosmetics, clothes, mineral tablets, a Thermos, books, a few pictures, his university diploma. When he had finished packing, he stood for a moment, gazing into the fluorescent lights he had ordered installed in his ceiling.

Later he sat at his kitchen table where he composed a short note to Monica. "I'm sorry for the pain I've caused you," he wrote. "I must go home now. I love you." He placed the note into an envelope, then stamped and sealed the letter.

He phoned for a taxi. When it came, he pulled on a topcoat, felt in his pocket for the gun he had learned to carry, and with his luggage and the briefcase departed his apartment.

At O'Hare airport Gabe purchased a ticket.

"Poor time to go to Phoenix," an airline clerk idly remarked as he checked Gabriel's luggage. "Just when summer is getting a good start here."

"Yes," Gabe said.

Episode 12

Gabriel Knapp arrived at Phoenix airport at 5 P.M. June 25. Immediately upon entering the terminal he telephoned Jacob Lockwood.

"This is Gabe," he said when he heard his friend's voice. "I'm here in Phoenix. I just got in."

There was a pause.

"What the hell did you say to Dan?" Jacob responded finally. "He's got half of Adamsville convinced you're a heretic."

Gabriel shook his head, shifted his weight. "We just got talking," he explained into the mouthpiece. "I thought maybe I could make him understand." Abruptly Gabriel changed his manner. "Listen," he said, "I've got to get home. They're on to me. I was fired yesterday."

"We can't send anyone for you, Gabe. It's too rough out there. All our posers are home now. No one goes out."

"How's the border? Can I get in?"

"We had some shots fired again yesterday. They're coming from all over now. A group came down from San Francisco last week, threatening to burn S.T.I. They left a pipe bomb near the guard shelter at the south gate." Jacob paused. "You'll have to be very careful," he advised.

"Which is the safest gate?" Gabe asked.

"The north one, I think."

"I have to get in tonight," Gabe said anxiously. "Can I make it through?"

"The FBI is at the south gate," Jacob said. "They're supposed to keep order and protect us. The state patrol is up at the north gate. They should help you get in safely. You haven't broken any laws, have you?"

Gabe laughed aloud at the naïveté of the question.

"I mean *besides* the rescue. You know they can't trace that to you. You didn't leave any evidence."

"Yeah," Gabe responded weakly. By now, he thought to himself, they knew that he had called in sick Wednesday, June 28, 2026.

"Listen, Gabe," Jacob's voice suddenly quickened. "Larry's insisting we don't let you in. He says you've relinquished your right to membership in the community."

"That's impossible! I'm green!"

"Larry says heretics cannot be members of the colony."

Key concepts:
Minority group
Prejudice
Discrimination

"What do the Elders say?" Gabriel asked.
"They want to let you in. They know you don't have anywhere else to go."
"Well, who's in control there, for God's sake?" Gabriel demanded nervously.
"Elderhome, officially," Jacob answered, then changed his tone. "Listen, I'll do all I can. I'll phone Elderhome now and have them okay your entry with the guards at the north gate."
Gabriel hung up. He collected his baggage and walked to a coffee shop where he purchased a carton of milk from a vending machine. He walked to a booth where he rented an automobile, later tossed his cases into the trunk, and—checking his rearview mirror often—left the airport.
As Gabe drove toward Adamsville, he smiled at the strength of the Arizona sunshine. In many respects it would be good to get home, he thought. No longer would he pretend he was something that he was not in order to gain employment or friends.
Knapp proceeded along Highway 60 through Fort Apache Indian Reservation, eventually entering St. Johns, Arizona. He was reminded of the two brutal murders his people had suffered there many years before. David and his sister Mary had not been murdered because they had done anything wrong, he knew from history. They had been beaten to death because David's skin was green.
As Gabe progressed still closer to Adamsville, he noted the increasing number of vehicles and pedestrians along the road. Here and there crowds gathered. People were yelling to one another. Some carried clubs. A few displayed rifles. Gabe drove ahead, keeping his eyes on the highway in front of him. His hands had begun to sweat. "You waited too long," he admonished himself aloud.
But when he finally approached the north gate to Adamsville, he found himself greeted by a single state patrolman. Gabe parked the car he had driven several yards from the entrance and removed his suitcases from the trunk. He intended to leave the car there. Once safely inside he would telephone the rental agency, informing them of the vehicle's whereabouts.

The patrolman whom Gabe had seen as he neared the gate approached. "Going somewhere?" the officer asked abruptly.

"Sir," Gabe stammered, "I live here."

"The hell you do!" the other guffawed. "Only greenfaces live in there." He took hold of Gabriel's arm. "Come on," he urged, "why don't you just go on home. They aren't hurtin' you any right now. They're monsters, I have to admit, but so far, at least, I have to protect them. That's my job."

Gabriel Knapp's mind had stopped at the term "greenfaces." He had never heard the expression before. Insulted to a degree he had not previously experienced, he felt himself resist the strength of the trooper's grip.

"Listen, buddy," the officer went on, "I've got to insist you don't go any closer to that gate. I hate them too, you know what I mean? I've got little kids too. You think I want them out kidnapping and killing little kids? But so far the law says I've got to keep peace around here, so let's go."

"Sir," Gabe said meekly, 'I *am* one of them. If you would just take my name and relay it to the guards at the gate, they would verify it." He spoke with deferent politeness, having regained his composure.

"You?" the patrolman sneered. "You're one of those greenfaces? ... What's your name then?"

"Gabriel Knapp."

"That your car?"

"It's a rented car, sir."

The officer checked the vehicle's registration. "If you're one of them, I'm not going to let you take this automobile inside," the trooper said, reluctantly approaching the guards' shelter.

Gabriel waited, pacing. When the officer returned he said, "Okay. They say to let you through."

Carrying his briefcase and one suitcase, Gabe walked toward the gate as it opened electronically before him. Once he had set these inside the gate, he went back outside for the rest of his belongings and rushed into what he hoped was safety within Adamsville.

Inside he was met by Jacob Lockwood. The two old friends embraced one another.

"It's been a long time," Jacob said. "Come on, I'll take you into town."

Gabe threw his luggage into the back of Jacob's solar vehicle and got in. As they drove, Jacob said, "After you called from the airport I contacted Elderhome to tell them you were coming. You can stay with me for a while. Later they'll give you a place in the valley."

The valley had become populated during the previous fifteen years. Located on the outskirts of town, it housed only mutants with dull skin. Generally those in the valley worked at S.T.I's routine factory jobs or served as janitors, maintenance workers, and waste collectors. Valley residents raised goats, drinking their milk for supplement. Jacob drove awhile, not saying anything. Finally Gabriel broke the silence.

"It's almost time for light-break," he said, making conversation.

"Do you still practice light-break?" Jacob asked.

"It's difficult," Gabe explained, "when you're on the outside. I had trouble finding somewhere to go in downtown Chicago during my lunch hour."

Jacob said nothing.

"In the summertime I walked along the lake or in the parks," Gabe continued. "Cloudy days I just stayed in and maybe went to a lunch counter somewhere to get a glass of milk."

"Dan was right then. You're still taking supplement."

Gabriel didn't answer. He sensed the regret in his companion's voice.

"They have a word for that now—for greens who don't stop taking supplement." Jacob swallowed. "They call them 'milk-whites'."

Gabriel turned the phrase in his mind. He was a "milk-white" here, he thought, and out there a "greenface." He grimaced bitterly at the irony of it.

Suddenly Jacob slammed his foot against the brake pedal. The car came to a screeching halt. Gabe looked up to see several men and women in the road ahead. They all wore face masks.

Before he realized what was happening, three greens pulled him from the auto and threw him to the ground. He felt a blow to the middle of his back. He was pummeled about the face and head. Someone kicked him in the side.

Jacob had attempted to protect his passenger, but could not. He was being held by two of the attackers. The blows to Gabe's body continued until Gabe lost consciousness.

When he awoke he was in Adamsville Hospital. A physician stood over him.

"Hello, Gabriel," he said sympathetically.

Gabe blinked. His chest hurt; his head throbbed. His body felt crushed, broken.

"You have some fractured ribs," the doctor was saying, "along with many lacerations and bruises. We stitched up a long gash on your head. We'll tape those ribs in place and soon you'll be able to get around."

Gabe nodded and fell asleep.

During the days that he remained in the hospital, he was visited once by Ruth Jones-the-Elder. "You came home," she said simply, entering his room.

"Yes, Elder," Gabe responded, his jaw aching.
"We are sorry about what happened here," Ruth said.
Gabe did not respond.
"Jacob says they all wore masks," Ruth continued. "He knows it was Larry Jones and some others, but he didn't actually see that it was Larry." She paused. "Did you see any of their faces?"
"No," Gabe murmured.
"I'm sorry," Ruth repeated. Then, changing the subject, she said, "According to the law, you must make a public confession."
"I know."
"We have scheduled it for July 2. Your physician says you will be well enough by then." Ruth smiled firmly. "And of course you will mature at the autumnal equinox," she added.
Gabe nodded.
"There's a vacant apartment in the valley," the Elder said then. "You may move into it when you like." She rose to leave. "Now," she said, "I'll let you get some sleep."

○ ○ ○

When Bradley Duncan left the conference on human mutations he had addressed May 10, he returned to his office at American University. There he began to prepare a paper that he would mail to Elderhome.

The Elders had allowed him to stay in Adamsville partially because they hoped that his observations would help them solve their internal problems. Consequently, he would offer the Elders what insights he could.

Duncan's eventual correspondence suggested that Adamsville posers who had shown themselves disloyal by putting off participation in the maturation ceremony had done so because going home often offered the prospect of downward mobility.

Duncan suggested that the belief that mutants did not physically mature because they had harbored thoughts of disloyalty proved a "self-fulfilling prophecy." A poser who waited in disappointment while his skin did not change color would eventually question the wisdom of his return home. To return meant to accept a position of low rank and general humiliation.

As a solution Duncan suggested that posers who did not become luminous be considered equal to their fellows. They would return more readily, he wrote, if they could participate in the maturing ceremony without feelings of inferiority—and if after the ceremony they could hold positions of honor, trust, and prestige.

Finally, Duncan pointed out that for Adamsvillers to define dull skin as evidence of inward disloyalty could actually be dysfunctional to the community. Dull greens were men and women of experience and expertise in many diverse fields. They might act as public relations persons or sales representatives for S.T.I., or as ambassadors to foreign nations, or lobbyists in Washington, D.C., or state capitals. Because they could travel more inconspicuously than their green fellows, they could do many things that were now left to young posers with little business or political experience.

The Elders received Duncan's paper on July 1, 2027.

Gabriel left Adamsville Hospital on June 30, five days after his attack. He went to stay with Jacob until he had fully recovered and could move into the valley apartment.

On July 2, the day scheduled for his public confession, Gabriel bathed, dressed, and walked with Jacob to the park.

The Elders had declared a religious holiday. Already a crowd of several hundred had formed. Gabe recognized Larry Jones; Daniel Adamson; Jacob's cousin, Rebecca Lockwood; and other bright greens standing together in one section of the sacred space.

The Elders had ascended to the ceremonial platform. Pain shot through Gabe's torso as he approached the same platform. At the microphone he spoke to the crowd.

"I am standing before you now," he began, his stomach growing sick with both humiliation and pain, "because I have sinned by disloyalty. I have refused to mature spiritually and therefore my skin has not matured physically." He swallowed, clenching his fists as they hung at his sides. "I come before you now," he forced the words, "to beg forgiveness."

Then suddenly the audience witnessed an unprecedented and surprising sequence of events. Michael and Ruth Jones-the Elder moved closer to Gabriel and kissed him on each cheek.

"Gabriel Knapp should not have been required to request public forgiveness," Michael said. "He came to us last year a rescuer and a hero."

The crowd murmured.

"He will not live in the valley," Ruth proclaimed.

Many in the crowd shouted angrily. Gabriel had chosen a life of collaboration with ungreens, they raved. For that there was only lasting humiliation.

The Elders motioned for quiet. Still the angry voices in the throng rumbled. "He is a milk-white," they jeered. "Milk-whites will destroy Adamsville!"

Episode 13

Thunderstorms drenched Chicago July 4, 2027. The American University faculty sailboat regatta which was to take place in Lake Michigan had to be canceled. Instead, faculty members and friends milled about the university campus. Louise, Brad, and Connie and their spouses gathered near the bowling lanes in the university student center. With them were Monica and several friends she had met through her membership in Civil Liberty for All.

Brad lowered his right knee and let go of the bowling ball. "Strike!" he roared, jumping up. "This beats flies and mosquitoes any day." He penciled his score onto the scoresheet. "Actually I'm glad it rained. I hate picnics."

"It's un-American to hate picnics, Bradley," Constance joked, scooping up a handful of salted, roasted soybeans. "It's deviant behavior."

Monica's thoughts had meanwhile turned to Gabriel. She had received the note he had written her his last day in Chicago. He would have been nervous and fidgety, Monica noted now, on a day like today. Rain always irritated him.

Louise Roanoke understood the shadow that had spread across her niece's face. "He'll be safer in Adamsville," Dr. Roanoke said, reading the younger woman's thoughts.

During the months that Monica had refused to see Gabe, she had been active with both former and new friends. While immediately after the termination of their relationship, Gabriel had occupied virtually all Monica's thoughts, she found that as the months progressed her mind turned to him less frequently.

When she did think of him, it was often his involvement in the Lake Hospital kidnapping that was foremost in her thoughts. She wondered about the victimized mother of the stolen infant; she wondered how the baby himself was getting along in Adamsville.

Now she said—more to herself than to anyone in the group—"I don't think I will ever respect him again after the kidnapping."

Key concepts:
Deviance
Labeling
Cultural relativity vs. ethnocentrism

"But he doesn't see the rescue as a crime, Monica," Bradley Duncan offered. "In Gabriel's culture what he did was not wrong but something to be admired."

"Kidnapping ought to be wrong in any culture," Monica replied. She placed her thumb and fingers into a bowling ball.

Connie Batterson joined the conversation. "Monica," she said, "you're a member of CLA now. Would you defend Gabe if he were arrested for the kidnapping?"

"He would deserve the best possible defense he could get," Monica said. "But that doesn't lessen the fact that stealing babies from their parents is wrong."

"Only because some people have decided it is," Brad said flatly, then hurled a heavy ball onto the alley before him.

"And because to permit kidnapping would be harmful to society," Louise added. She raised the ball until it was level with her chin, looking past it intently to the three pins she would drop for a spare.

"Kidnapping is wrong because those who are in power see it as wrong and have the strength to impose their morality upon others," Connie suggested.

Monica slammed her bowling ball onto the rack beside her. "Sometimes I get sick of this sociological game playing," she exploded suddenly. "Kidnapping is wrong because it's wrong, that's all. It's a lousy, rotten, criminal thing to do!"

Louise rushed to her niece, wrapping her arm around Monica's shoulder.

Batterson spoke. "I'm sorry, Monica. Really. I guess we sociologists forget how much our professional objectivity can irritate people."

Duncan scurried to a portable bar on the other side of the room and returned with two beers. He handed one to Monica. "Here," he said, "let's drink to the Fourth of July. I'm sorry."

◉ ◉ ◉

The strong odor of gunpowder assaulted Gabriel's nostrils as he made his way from Adamsville cemetery toward the community's southern entrance. It was the Fourth of July, and Gabe expected the air near the entrance to be heavy with gunpowder. Yet the smell frightened him. He wondered how he would know as he stood guard during the night whether the explosive claps he heard were innocent fireworks or shots aimed toward his colony.

Two days earlier, on the afternoon of Gabriel's public confession, Larry Jones had successfully insisted that Knapp be assigned night guard duty at the south gate.

Jones had followed Ruth and Michael to Elderhome after watching in horror their performance at Gabriel's public confession. He had found his great aunt and uncle seated in the front parlor.

"Why did you do such a thing?" he had demanded. "What you said from that platform was against everything Adam stood for. It was wrong!"

Ruth handed Larry Duncan's sociological report. Slowly Larry had read it. Finally he asked, his voice loud with anger, "Why did you let them come here? Adam never allowed outsiders in! Why did you do it?" Larry grew furious, shaking his fist. "Now you're following their advice! Your foolish collaboration with these—these protein-consuming social scientists—goes against all Adam taught!" The Elders remained calm, showing almost no reaction.

His anger increasing, Larry waved the report at them. "So this is why you made a mockery of the public confession? This is what led you to announce that Knapp won't have to live in the valley?"

"We studied the paper for several hours before doing what we did," Michael had said.

"We decided not to cancel Gabriel's confession, but to use it as an opportunity to demonstrate that Adamsville would begin to rethink its policy concerning dull greens."

Larry's voice grew sullen. "So you've begun to let ungreens tell you what's good for greens," he sneered. "If you plan to let Knapp live outside the valley," he said, "then I'm going to insist he take duty at one of the gates."

"He has considerable managerial experience," Ruth had ventured. "We thought we could use him at S.T.I. Perhaps after the furor over his rescue mission recedes, he could even travel for us."

Larry Jones glared. "I've got a lot of people on my side," he said coldly. "If you refuse to assign Knapp guard duty, I promise you your authority will be seriously challenged."

The next day Gabriel received an official communiqué from Elderhome. Gabe was invited to move into a glass fourplex located near the center of Adamsville. It was a habitat until now reserved for bright greens.

Also, the message read, Gabe was to replace a not-yet-matured young green named Peter Adamson as night guard at the south entrance beginning the next day, July 4.

Now Gabriel walked nervously toward his first night's watch. It was 4:30 P.M. He was scheduled to begin duty at 5.

Gabe had spent the earlier part of the afternoon at Adamsville cemetery, sitting beside Jonathan's simple headstone. Still aching from the blows he had suffered the previous week, he had gone to the graveyard to keep a belated vigil for the soft parent whom he had loved very much.

He sat quietly for a long time near the grave, soaking in the reality of Jonathan's death. He would have liked to ask Jonathan's forgiveness for his negligence as a son. Tears had filled Gabriel's eyes.

Sometime during the vigil Loretta Larson, Gabe's stern parent, approached. She had come to bring some desert flowers to place near Jonathan's grave.

"What are you doing here?" she had asked, startled. It was the first time since Gabe's return that she had spoken to him face to face.

"Just thinking, I guess," Gabriel said. "I miss him."

"You're too late for the vigil, you know. You didn't come home when you should have."

Gabriel had said nothing.

"Jonathan talked about you often, especially after the rescue last year. He was very fond of you, you know."

"I didn't know he was dead until Dan came," Gabe said. "Why didn't you call me when he died? I would have come for the vigil."

"Gabriel," Loretta said, "Adamsville has not ignored you. You have ignored Adamsville."

Gabe looked into the woman's face. "Remember how well we used to get along, you and me?"

Loretta studied Gabriel. "I'm told you still drink supplement," she said.

"Why does that have to matter?" Gabriel had demanded, suddenly desperate in his fear that the isolation he had known on the outside might continue in Adamsville.

"Drinking supplement at your age is a sign of disloyalty, Gabriel,"

Loretta reminded. She turned to leave. "It's wrong," she had added, walking away.

The conversation between Gabe and Loretta Larson had taken place hours before. Now Gabe entered the glass-roofed guard shelter. "How's it been?" he asked Ann Sullivan, the mutant he was to relieve.

Ann Sullivan was a chlorophyllic of fifty-three whose skin had never become more than faintly green. She lived in the valley, sharing an apartment with two other dull greens. Always tired and considered lazy, Ann was one of Adamsville's least valued citizens. While she had matured ceremonially when she was twenty-seven, the fact that the color of her skin remained dull was taken as a sign that she persisted in some sort of disloyalty.

Ann looked up at Gabriel. She said, "Some people came around yelling 'Kill the greenfaces'. And a lot of fireworks have been going off. But otherwise it's been pretty quiet." She rose to leave. "Well," she said slowly, "I guess I'll be going on home."

Gabriel sat down in the chair which Ann had vacated. He set a sack which he had carried onto the table in front of him. From it he pulled his Thermos and poured himself a cup of milk.

"Can I have a swig of that?" Ann asked. "It's a long walk home, and I'm feeling a little weak."

"Are you sick?" Gabe noted that she looked faint.

"I don't think so," Ann responded. Gabriel offered her the milk he had poured. "From one milk-white to another," he said, pleased to be talking with a fellow dull green. "Now go home and get some rest."

"Thanks," she smiled. She swallowed the milk and was gone.

Gabe Knapp placed the palms of his hands against the sides of his body, applying gentle pressure to his aching ribs. Several hours passed. Loneliness crept into the shelter with the lengthening shadows. The pain in his jaw and ribs only accentuated his feelings of desolation.

He dug into his pockets for cigarettes. There was no place to buy them in Adamsville; greens did not smoke. He planned to quit what he knew was a bad habit when those he had brought with him from the outside were gone. Finding a rumpled package, he lit one of his few remaining smokes.

A car neared the gate. From the passenger window someone hurled an empty bottle. Seconds later Gabriel heard the squeal of tires and the evening was quiet.

For reasons which Gabriel didn't understand, his thoughts turned to the chromosomal mother of the infant he had rescued. It had been reported in the papers that she had suffered a nervous breakdown. Perhaps the rescues were wrong. Sometimes anyway. Perhaps Monica was right after all.

Knapp poured himself a cup of milk from the Thermos. He was convinced now that what he had suggested to Daniel when the two had talked in his Chicago apartment was true. Religious loyalty had nothing at all to do with the color of his skin. He resolved to talk with Ann Sullivan about it soon.

It had grown dark. Three cars approached the gate from the outside. Their headlights went out. Gabe heard car doors open and shut, followed by approaching voices and footsteps. He stood, grabbing a solar laser projector from its position on the wall beside him.

The outsiders came closer.

"This is a lynch mob!" one of them yelled. Gabe heard them laugh.

He stepped from the shelter. "This is private property," he said. "If you come any closer, you'll be trespassing."

"Greenfaces don't own nothing but what they can steal," the response pierced the darkness.

"The state patrol is out there," Gabriel called. "They'll arrest you."

"We passed them down the road," someone answered. "They didn't pay us no attention."

"Stop!" Knapp shouted into the darkness. "I have a solar weapon. I'll shoot."

Suddenly one of them grabbed him from behind. Pain screeched through Gabe's body as he felt new blows to his already hurting ribs. The laser projector was knocked from his hand and lost in the darkness.

Someone grabbed Gabriel's ankles. Another held his arms, while still a third hit him about the head and chest.

"Hey, greenface," he heard one of them taunt, "how many babies have you stolen?"

"Hey, greeeeeeeeenie," another called, "it's the Fourth of July. Want to help us celebrate the Fourth of July?"

Half conscious, Gabriel vaguely perceived the arrival of a fourth vehicle. Two state police officers stepped out. A spotlight glared, flooding the area. As Gabriel lay limp on the sandy ground, he felt his attackers pulled away from him.

Later he was handcuffed along with the others. He felt himself being helped into the back seat of an automobile.

"We're taking you all in to St. Johns," one of the agents was saying. "We'll contact headquarters in Phoenix and decide what to do with all of you then."

At the tiny St. Johns police station, Gabe was escorted to a long, wooden bench. He sat across the room from his attackers. Bruised and bleeding, he felt himself growing sick to his stomach. He wished they would turn on more lights.

An officer approached. "What's your name?" he asked.

"Gabriel Knapp."

"You a resident of Adamsville?"

Gabe nodded. The officer left. When he returned a few minutes later, he said, "We're booking the others for disturbing the peace."

Gabe looked up. "Can I go home?" he asked. "They can take care of me in the hospital at home."

"Not if you're Gabriel Knapp," came the reply. "You're wanted for kidnapping."

Episode 14

Gabriel Knapp's trial opened in Chicago October 1, 2027. Monica Roanoke represented him. When Gabriel phoned her from Phoenix July 5, she had first suggested she find him another attorney, explaining that she knew several qualified lawyers who would take his case. But Gabe had insisted she defend him herself. With mixed emotions she had agreed.

Knapp had been held without bond. On July 29, still in custody, he was sent to Illinois where subsequently he spent nearly two months in Cook County jail awaiting trial.

Because a large majority of prospective jurors admitted upon questioning that they had already reached a conclusion regarding Knapp's guilt, attorneys took nine days to choose a jury.

Gabriel's arrest in Phoenix July 4 had sparked an increase in national violence. On July 10 a truck loaded with S.T.'s heading for an automobile factory in Detroit was hijacked and set ablaze near Battle Creek.

Meanwhile rumors had sprung up in and around Denver that members of a commune west of that city were descendents of a second kind of mutants. Commune members, many believed, were mentally deficient monsters whose pastimes included torture and mutilation of animals and children.

On July 29, 2027, several persons from Denver joined activists from Steamboat Springs, Aspen, Colorado Springs, and Vail. The mob converged upon the suspected commune, set fire to the main house, and fatally stabbed and shot the twenty-five women, men, and children who resided there.

The following day, in a separate incident, three homemade bombs exploded simultaneously in the Phoenix airport, killing fifteen and injuring thirty. Concerned Citizens for National Defense claimed responsiblity for that act of terrorism.

On August 2 a Union Pacific railroad train carrying S.T.'s to East Coast factories was purposely derailed near Des Moines. The engineer was shot four times in the head.

By the end of August most major cities had summoned state national guards. Federal infantry divisions were stationed in New York, Los Angeles, San Francisco, Chicago, St. Louis, and Phoenix.

Key concepts:
Collective behavior
Social movements

Meanwhile the periodic border disturbances that had plagued Adamsville for nearly ten years had intensified. FBI personnel, although their numbers had been substantially increased, found it increasingly difficult to maintain order near the colony's gates.

Inside Adamsville Larry Jones insisted that S.T.I impose a boycott immediately, refusing to market its solar transistors within the United States. The national economy, he reasoned, having grown increasingly dependent upon S.T.'s, could not survive without them for longer than a few days. Once Adamsville held outsiders in this economic vise, greens would be in a position to voice their demands: the establishment of a separate and independent green nation, consisting of what now were the states of Arizona and New Mexico.

The Elders, on the other hand, procrastinated, fearing that to impose the boycott might further limit Gabriel's already tenuous chance for a fair trial. Furthermore, they refused to see the future of Adamsville in terms of a separate nation.

On August 10 the epidemic upheaval that troubled the nation outside infected Adamsville itself. A tiny solar explosive device, manufactured at S.T.I., was discovered upon the steps to Elderhome. The device had been placed there by some of the community's radical militarists.

Hundreds of miles to the east the faculty at American University on Lake Michigan had been placed under heavy security. Sociologists and other faculty members had received telephoned threats to their homes. Duncan, Roanoke, Batterson, and several others had been assigned personal bodyguards.

The night of October 5, four days after Gabriel's trial opened, 200 vigilantes battled with FBI agents outside Adamsville's gates. While many hurled grenades, fashioned from pop bottles and tin cans, others struggled with green guards. Amid the chaos two ungreens managed to sneak into Adamsville. Before they escaped the two had murdered three greens. The murders would not be discovered by residents until the following morning. Dead were Rebecca Lockwood, Leonard Decker, chromosomal father of the infant Gabe had taken from Lake Hospital, and their sixteen-month-old rescued son.

Members of the press, now permanently camped near Adamsville, reported the killings the following morning. Gabriel learned of the murders from a United States marshal who escorted him from his cell to the courtroom.

Gabe sat pale and unresponsive through that morning. Shortly before noon he asked Monica to request a short recess so that he could go to the rest room. Once inside the lavatory, he lay his head into a washbasin and heaved, first liquid and then nothing, until finally he was taken, limp and perspiring, to his cell. The court remained adjourned—a jury still not selected—until October 8.

On October 6 Solar Transistors, Inc., shut down. Ruth and Michael Jones-the-Elder had consented to impose the boycott. Three of their people had been murdered in cold blood. Some action had to be taken—in spite of the possible repercussions the decision might have upon Gabriel's trial. Wall Street brokers predicted a crash within thirty days should the boycott continue. Power companies along the Eastern Seaboard, having grown dependent upon solar transistors, cut down production, causing brownouts from Florida to Maine.

Threats of violence enveloped Chicago and the federal courts building October 11 as Monica began her opening statement.

"Ladies and gentlemen," she began, assuming a position close to the jury box, "the prosecution has promised to prove that the defendent, Gabriel Knapp, sneaked into Lake Hospital June 28, 2026, kidnapped an infant from the second-floor nursery, then boarded a plane and flew with the child to Phoenix, ultimately delivering the victim to an Arizona community known as Green Colony or Adamsville.

"The prosecution must have facts to support this argument! . . . I beg you to remember your obligations as members of this jury. You are commissioned with two equally important responsibilities: One is to see that justice is done in this specific case; the other is to assure that this nation's legal system is neither sacrificed nor weakened. . . . We must not forget that if we deny the full benefits of the law to Mr. Knapp today, then another jury can more readily deny *you* those same benefits tomorrow. . . . We cannot convict Mr. Knapp simply because we believe he is green."

Monica was seated next to Gabe. "This is a political trial," she whispered to her client.

The prosecution called as its first witness the vice president in charge of personnel from Chicago National. He testified that he knew Knapp to be a green. He had discovered such, he said, on June 22,

2027, when he received a letter from a physician who had examined Gabriel one year before.

Monica objected on the grounds that what transpires during a physician-patient relationship is privileged information, and therefore the doctor's letter was inadmissible. The court sustained her objection and advised the jurors to ignore the testimony.

Next the prosecution called Garcia, the agent who had followed Daniel Adamson to Gabriel's apartment. She testified that she had tailed a young man from Adamsville to Chicago where on the evening of March 14, 2027, he spent two hours with the defendant in his apartment. Garcia testified further that upon leaving Knapp's apartment, the young visitor had returned directly to Adamsville.

On cross-examination Monica asked, "Do you *know*, Ms. Garcia, whether Mr. Knapp is a green?"

"I know that he was visited by one."

"But you do not know that he himself is a green, isn't that correct?"

"Yes," Ms. Garcis said.

During the next several days the prosecution called twenty-three witnesses, all of them minor acquaintances of Gabriel Knapp. They testified that he often refused or skipped meals, that many times they had heard him complain about the dim lighting in a room, that he seemed always to want the lights turned up as far a they would go, and that he generally "acted a little different."

Gabriel's secretary, Mr. Jacobs, testified that often he saw his boss drink milk, but couldn't recall ever seeing him eat anything solid. Jacobs testified also that he had watched Knapp grow increasingly nervous over the past year and a half, "especially since the day he received the report of his physical."

Monica had already determined that her client would not take the stand. She would simply rebut the facts presented, ultimately arguing that the prosecution had presented insufficient evidence for conviction.

On the seventh day of testimony the prosecution called the FBI agent who had read Knapp's file compiled at Chicago National Insurance Company. He testified that, according to information from that file, Gabriel had called in sick the morning of June 28, 2026, complaining of a "summer cold."

Monica rose for cross-examination. "Do you know for sure," she demanded, "that Mr. Knapp was *not* home suffering from a cold June 28, 2026?"

"No," the witness responded, "not absolutely for sure."

"It is entirely possible, then, as far as you know, that Mr. Knapp stayed home from work June 28 because he was ill with a cold, is it not?"

"Yes," the agent muttered, "it's possible."

Later the prosecution called the Lake Hospital nurse who had directed Gabriel to the nursery. Producing a tan jacket and wig recovered by police from the rest room of a filling station across the street from Lake Hospital, the district attorney asked whether the witness had seen either of the items before.

The nurse said she couldn't be sure, but perhaps the jacket looked familiar. Gabriel was ordered to put on the jacket and wig.

"Is that the man who asked directions to the nursery?"

"I can't be sure," the nurse replied.

While Monica fought for Gabe's freedom in court, the attention of those outside the courtroom had been diverted to the nation's economic crisis. The stock market had plummeted. Newpapers, politicians, labor leaders, and industry alike predicted returning depression. By the time Gabriel's trial had reached the seventh day of testimony, Adamsville's Elders had made their demands nationally understood. The Associated Press, in a story datelined "Adamsville," reported on October 19 that unless colony representives were invited to attend and vote at the upcoming conference on human mutations, S.T.I. would not resume manufacture of solar transistors.

On October 20, the eighth day of testimony in Gabriel's trial, the prosecution called Bradley Duncan.

"State your full name," the prosecuting attorney said when Brad had seated himself in the witness chair.

"Bradley Clarence Duncan."

"Your occupation?"

"Sociologist."

"You spent several months in Green Colony, did you not?"

"In Adamsville. Yes."

"Did you spend the afternoon of June 28, 2026, in Green Colony?"

"In Adamsville; yes, I did."

"Will you tell this court, Mr. Duncan, what took place"—the attorney hesitated—"in Adamsville the afternoon of June 28, 2026?"

Duncan cleared his throat. "I cannot answer that question," he said. "It is privileged information." The judge ordered Duncan to answer the question. The sociologist persisted in his refusal. Fifteen minutes later he was sentenced to ten days in Cook County jail for contempt of court.

The prosecution then called Dr. Constance Batterson and, later, Dr. Louise Roanoke, who likewise refused to testify and were similarly sentenced.

Later that afternoon the prosecution called a representative from the U.S. Department of the Interior. She testified that her special area of expertise included knowledge of green culture patterns and that she knew for certain that under some circumstances greens believed in kidnapping infants.

The next day the prosecution summoned to the stand the steward who had hosted Gabriel on his June 28 flight from Chicago to Phoenix. The steward testified that he had seen a man resembling Gabe with a newborn infant aboard US-Russian Airlines Flight No. 742.

Monica cross-examined the witness. "What was the passenger who carried the baby wearing that day?"

The steward said he could not be sure.

"How was the baby wrapped?" Monica asked.

"In a blanket, I think."

"What color was the blanket?"

"I don't remember for sure."

"You are quite certain that this is the gentleman whom you hosted, but you don't know what he had on or how the baby he supposedly carried was dressed?"

"I know that the man with the baby looked like that man," the steward pointed toward Gabriel.

"But you can't be absolutely certain that this *is* the man, can you?"

"Not absolutely certain."

On October 23, the day before Monica would deliver her closing argument, the U.S. secretary of the interior consented to the mutant's demands. Furthermore, at Adamsville's subsequent insistence, the conference was scheduled six months earlier than had been previously planned. Delegates to the conference would meet in Omaha November 15, 2027.

Monica Roanoke began her closing argument October 24, 2027. "Ladies and gentlemen of the jury," she announced, "this is a political trial. My client is not on trial here as a human being who has transgressed the law, but as a representative of a group hated and feared within our society.

"The prosecution has attempted to prove that Mr. Knapp is a chlorophyllic. Because of that—and only because of that—he is charged here with a serious federal crime. . . . This morning the prosecution has based its closing argument on two things primarily: that Mr. Knapp is a chlorophyllic and that chlorophyllics believe in something they call rescuing. I am not here to argue these two assertions, nor am I here to argue that I believe kidnapping is ever honorable. I am simply here to remind you that these two assertions alone are not sufficient evidence to convict Mr. Knapp of the Lake Hospital crime. There are no facts sufficient to convince us beyond a reasonable doubt that Gabriel Knapp kidnapped an infant."

The jury deliberated two days before agreeing that the prosecution had failed to prove defendent Gabriel Knapp guilty.

Episode 15

Gabriel evidenced almost no emotion when the jury foreman pronounced the verdict, "Not guilty." He was exhausted. The child for whom he had risked his life had been brutally murdered. The baby's chromosomal mother remained under treatment in a Chicago mental hospital. While Monica had defended Gabe illustriously, she had simultaneously dashed any hopes he had nursed for resuming their previous relationship. His ribs and skull sometimes still ached from the injuries he had suffered several months before.

The courtroom emptied. Gabriel sat quietly in the place he had occupied throughout the trial, staring at his clasped hands. Monica stood next to him.

"You're free now," she forced, breaking the long silence between them.

"Yes," Gabe nodded. "Thank you." Suddenly he added, "I'm sorry for all the deception before."

Monica leaned toward Gabe and kissed him. "Take care," she whispered, then turned to leave the courtroom.

It was 1 P.M. when the wire services reported Knapp's acquittal. Demonstrations both for and against the verdict erupted across the country. Later that afternoon, however, Gabriel would return to Adamsville without incident.

Using a pseudonym and accompanied by four secret service agents, he flew to Tucson. From there he was driven in a government limousine to the colony.

Gabe remained silent during most of the journey. Occasionally he poured milk from his Thermos, gulping it, hoping to replenish temporarily his waning strength. "A greenface on the outside," the words nagged him as he rode, "and a milk-white at home."

Two miles outside Adamsville's southern entrance, Arizona state authorities stopped the car. Only after Knapp's escorts had convinced

Key concepts:
Social conflict
Class conflict
Social change

---

the local officers of their identities was the party allowed to proceed.

This heightened security was new to Gabriel. "No one within 2 miles of the borders now," one of the escorting officers explained. "New orders issued yesterday from Washington." The speaker grunted. "They don't want another boycott."

Minutes later the car stopped. Just ahead stretched the colony's south gate. "I'll get out here," Gabe said, reaching to open the door. The residents were expecting him: He had phoned Elderhome from Tucson.

Ann Sullivan advanced from within the guard shelter. "Gabe?" she called. "That you?"

"Yes." He moved quickly toward the electronic gate which had already begun to open. When he reached Ann, he took her hands. Although he didn't know the woman well, he had found himself thinking of her during his trial.

While the two stood facing one another, Gabriel attempted to assess his feelings about being home—wondering at the same time whether he could ever be really "home." Meanwhile the limousine in which he had arrived disappeared to the south, returning to Tucson.

"The Elders and Jacob Lockwood are here to greet you," Ann said. "Alexander brought them down. They're waiting a little way up the road. They'll take you into town."

Knapp and Sullivan walked northward a few hundred feet. When Ruth, Michael, and Jacob caught sight of Gabriel's advancing silhouette, the three rushed toward him.

Michael put his brilliant green arms around Knapp's neck. "Gabriel, Gabriel," he breathed, "you have suffered so much."

Ruth kissed Gabe on the cheek. "We're glad to welcome you back," she said. "We were very afraid that they would find you guilty —even without the evidence."

Gabriel said nothing. Unnoticed Ann Sullivan had returned to the guard shelter.

Michael said, "You won't take guard duty again. It was a mistake. You would not have been arrested if you had not taken guard duty."

"That's over now," Gabe murmured.

"Welcome home," Jacob said then, extending his lime green hand toward his friend. "We missed you."

"You had a fine attorney," Michael said. "You made a good choice."

"Yes." Gabriel looked down at his feet.

"You missed the autumnal equinox," Ruth smiled. "Three greens matured."

"I will mature at the spring ceremony," Gabriel assured them, again aware of his fatigue.

"We've moved your things into the house you were assigned before your arrest," Jacob said. Gabriel remembered: It was the large, glass house near central Adamsville. He stood quiet for several seconds.

"I would like to live in the valley," he announced softly. "I would be more comfortable there."

"That's ridiculous," Michael exclaimed.

Duncan's paper, which Elderhome had received July 1, had eroded their confidence in the belief that dull greens must be disloyal sinners. Now the Elders had come to view valleyites as victims of genetic misfortune. Knapp had suggested to Dan Adamson that failure to mature might be the result of a green's possessing fewer mutant chromosomes. It now seemed clear to the Elders—and to all the cooperationists—that valleyites were genetically inferior, and that explained their well-known tendency to disease.

"The valley people are often sick, Gabriel," Ruth reminded. "You would not enjoy living there."

"I am one of them," Gabriel responded.

"You have never appeared very ill to me," Jacob retorted. "You must have been fairly healthy to accomplish what you did at Chicago National."

"I am one of them," Gabriel insisted.

THE STORY OF ADAMSVILLE

Michael broke in. "Let's not discuss it now. Gabriel is exhausted. He's had a grueling experience. We're all emotionally drained. We'll consider this again in the morning."

"Gabriel," Jacob offered, "why don't you stay with me tonight? You can decide on this tomorrow."

The four entered the waiting limousine.

The following morning Gabriel came to realize to what extent dissent had come to pervade Adamsville. According to the agreement made between Elderhome and Washington, the colony would send three voting delegates to the third conference on human mutations. Who these representatives would be had grown into a major controversy.

All Adamsvillers agreed that to send the community's greenest members would not only be unnecessarily dangerous but also politically foolish. Ungreen delegates, shocked and startled at the sight of the mutants, would ignore any rational arguments these greens might pose.

The answer was to send either young, not-yet-matured mutants or dull greens from the valley. Gabriel found his people angrily divided upon which was the better solution.

Larry Jones and the radical militarists, still strongly convinced that failure to physically mature was evidence of spiritual transgression, argued that the only trustworthy delegates would come from the ranks of the young.

Elderhome, on the other hand, influenced by Duncan, held that older, more experienced mutants might perform better as delegates. Many dull greens had spent several years on the outside before their final return to the colony.

While it was true, Elderhome and the cooperationists argued, that valleyites tended to be physically weak and often ill, that fact did not necessarily lessen their potential as influential delegates. "We will choose the most experienced and best qualified of our valleyites," Ruth had summed up Elderhome's position, "and they will do a good job."

As residents took sides on this issue, the purpose for attending the conference became still another source of contention. Elderhome wanted a scientific resolution that photosynthetic creatures should be considered "just as human" as ungreens.

Larry Jones, however, argued that the delegation's role should be to dramatize S.T.I.'s political and economic threat. Adamsville, he often yelled from the platform in the community's public park, must demand establishment of a separate green nation, consisting of the present states of Arizona and New Mexico.

Simmering dissent threatened to erupt into a full boil when, on Sunday, November 2, 2027, Larry Jones again climbed the steps to the community's sacred platform. Gradually a crowd gathered, many of the onlookers armed with the guns Bradley Duncan had noted more than a year before.

"Tomorrow the Elders will choose our representatives," Larry called, his fists clenched and raised, his voice dramatically passionate. "Fellow greens, true followers of Adam, we cannot send our sinners! What people sends its lowest—those of whom it is ashamed—to represent them? Tell me! What government has ever purposefully commissioned people it could not trust to speak for it?"

The approximately fifty Adamsvillers to whom Larry spoke cheered. Others joined the crowd until, thirty minutes later, Jones bellowed his message to three hundred greens.

"Now I wonder," Larry thumped, "Just why Michael and Ruth govern Adamsville? Who is it that gave them such authority? Was it Adam Jones III, their father, my great-grandfather? Maybe—but we have no written documents to that effect. Adam left no specific rules for choosing who would govern after him. When he died he left a family, the beginnings of a nation—but not a nation.

"Who then decided that Michael and Ruth should govern us? *They* did!" Larry paused, allowing his audience to absorb his message. When he began again his voice was softer.

"And that was fine with all of us so long as the Elders followed the traditions and philosophy established by our prophet, Adam."

Gabriel and Jacob joined the crowd; Gabriel recognized his sister, Elizabeth, near the platform.

"But Ruth and Michael have not continued to follow Adam's wishes," Jones went on. "Not only have they allowed outsiders into Adamsville, but they have taken ungreens' advice! By their actions they have implied that outsiders apparently know better than we do what is good for us.

"In saying this they have sinned against our prophet and father, Adam. They have admitted that they do not really—genuinely—believe that our people are the future people of earth; for if they really believed this, they would trust their own judgments above those of outsiders!"

Gabe whispered to Jacob, "Will the Elders respond to this?"

"They may come to the park to make an official statement later," Jacob answered.

"Adam, our founder and prophet," Larry called, "established Adamsville as a separate colony. He discouraged his children from leaving the colony, and, later, he erected fences to ensure Adamsville's separatism. Why is it then that now Ruth and Michael refuse to follow this tradition of separatism? Are they afraid?"

Ann Sullivan and several others from the valley had wandered into the park. They collected near the rear of the cheering throng.

"This is no time to be afraid," Jones bellowed, "for we have already proven that we can bring American industry to its knees! Why then are the Elders afraid? Or is it that they are really not afraid: that really they are ashamed of their color and of their calling?"

The crowd had grown unruly. Larry flung his arms about him as he yelled his message, his face growing darker with increased emotion. It was as if a dam within him had broken; all the power welled up in him came rushing, washing through the crowd, carrying it along in deep, turbulent waves.

Spontaneously refueled by the crowd's collective response, Jones raised his voice. It was as if he gained strength from his followers' shouts of approval.

"Maybe," he screamed now, "maybe Michael and Ruth aim to surrender Adamsville! Perhaps they are traitors! I think—don't you—that they are ashamed of their sacred mutations. And that shame has caused them to plan to surrender all of us!"

Larry Jones had never gone this far before. The crowd grew suddenly quiet. The orator swallowed, then went on.

"This is why they want to send our least acceptable residents as delegates. This is why they plan to send disloyal sinners! Only the scum of our community could be persuaded to deliver us into the hands of our enemies. Only our most deceitful members, those milk-whites who harbor secret sins and who sometimes openly promote heresy, only these most despicable—"

The crowd rumbled.

"—only these would be capable of Elderhome's treasonous plan."

Larry paused momentarily, then shouted as with sudden vision. "Valleyites," he screeched, "are parasites!"

Suddenly the sound of a gunshot cracked the air. Amid the screaming and pushing that followed, Larry Jones fell to his knees. His right hand clutched his chest. Seconds later he was dead.

Unknown to anyone present, Ann Sullivan had in a moment of uncontrolled anger issued the fatal bullet.

Episode 16

Amid the thunder of national dissent, the third conference on human mutations opened November 15, 2027. Gabriel Knapp, Ann Sullivan, and Daniel Adamson made up the Adamsville delegation.

Gabe Knapp, milk-white heretic, had emerged as a leader among his people.

Seconds after Larry Jones was murdered, Gabriel had sped toward Elderhome. "Get the Elders," he had demanded, pushing past Mr. Alexander and into the front parlor. "Larry Jones has been shot!"

Withing seconds Ruth and Michael appeared.

"You'll have to come to the park," Gabriel had urged when he realized their shock and confusion. "You must quiet the radicals; we could have civil war by this afternoon!"

But both Ruth and Michael proved unequal to the challenge, and it was Gabe who succeeded in delivering his people from the crisis.

"This felled leader," Gabe had called from beside Jones's assassinated body, "will have a hero's burial . . ."

Steadily the crowd had grown quiet. While Jones's followers were both stunned and angered, no leader appeared from within their ranks. The radical cause, it seemed, would be severely weakened with Larry Jones's death.

On Tuesday, November 4, Gabriel requested a conference with Ruth and Michael.

"I think it would best serve Adamsville now," Gabriel proposed, "if you were to send to the conference two dull greens from the valley and one we consider a pure green, not yet physically matured."

The Elders hesitated. Then Ruth said, "Gabriel, would it be too dangerous for you to go?"

"Washington has pledged our delegates protection equal to what they give their president when he's away from the White House," Michael reminded her.

"I am planning to go," Gabriel said firmly. "I will take Ann Sullivan and Daniel."

"Ann Sullivan is sick and not up to this," Ruth said. "She is genetically impoverished."

"Ann is weak from malnutrition," Gabe replied, his jaw set. "Some of Adamsville's ways have not been good for her. She will go with me."

Ironically Larry Jones's untimely death had accomplished his own

Key concept:
Definition of the situation

---

driving purpose: The Elders had, during the crisis that followed, relinquished—although inadvertently—their authority.

Now, eleven days later, Louise Roanoke, Constance Batterson, and Bradley Duncan took their places among fellow conference members in the hotel auditorium. Tension, like summer humidity, hung in the room. Outside, secret service personnel guarded entrances. Beyond them milled groups of demonstrators. Occasionally the strained order erupted into violence as protesters confronted one another.

The conference would open in just a few minutes. "Monica didn't come then?" Constance asked Louise in an attempt to lighten the atmosphere. Louise shook her head, obviously relieved that her niece had chosen to remain in the relative safety of Chicago.

While Monica had entertained the notion of joining other CLA members in demonstrations at the conference, she had ultimately decided against it. Her presence, she reasoned, might serve to remind attending scientists of Gabriel's trial—and consequently of greens' political-religious conviction that kidnapping is sometimes honorable.

For the third time attending scientists watched and listened as the conference opened. "We have the unprecedented presence of three green delegates with us," the United States secretary of the interior was saying.

Upon introduction the delegation from Adamsville stood, turned to face the apprehensive audience. Daniel stared, stone-faced. Gabriel searched eyes, looking for faint glimmers of empathy. Ann smiled, aware that not even Gabriel knew to what extent his being in Omaha was a result of her own impulsive and angry action.

"*Are* they human, Brad?" Louise whispered to Duncan, seated next to her. "In your objective, detached, scientific judgment?"

"There is no such thing," Duncan chuckled under his breath.

Constance Batterson had overheard the exchange.

"Go to hell," she sneered good-naturedly to Brad.

"Mr. Knapp," the secretary of the interior was explaining, "will address this conference first . . . "

Soon Gabe approached the podium. He stood for a time in silence. When he opened his mouth, the words fluttered. "I'm nervous," he said, managing a smile. "It's a human quality."

The audience murmured.

"Some of my people," Gabe said in clear tones now, "Believed that we should come here with threats."

The attending scientists shuffled.

"But that's not why I'm here," Gabriel continued. "I'm here rather to suggest that from a scientific, genetic, and evolutionary point of view, we green photosynthesizers are the answer—or can be the answer—to world food shortages . . .

"Adamsvillers who possess so much chlorophyll within their skin that their flesh is green virtually never need to ingest protein. In sufficiently lighted environments, they can live by drinking only water.

"Greens like myself whose skin does not contain that much chlorophyll exist with varying levels of required food intake. Throughout my lifetime I have ingested milk and little else . . .

"It seems to us, esteemed scientists, that whatever your distaste for us, we are the most promising hope for surviving the next century on this planet. We mutants are in the evolutionary sense a messianic breed who must be allowed to multiply throughout earth in order that humankind will not starve to death. But in order to save this species we must be considered human beings."

To many Gabe's was an illustrious presentation. Some few stood in applause.

Would greens be defined as human beings? Discussion and debate ravaged the group for days. Biochemists were spilt on the issue. Economists warned of the danger posed by the ever-present possibility of further S.T. boycotts. A historian asked whether officially to define greens as human beings wouldn't serve to legitimate their "violent attacks upon infants and young children."

Louise Roanoke answered that once the mutants were permitted to live openly—no longer posing and free to communicate their mutation to future mates—rescuing would no longer serve as a manifest function for greens. What latent functions the practice filled could be performed by various, less threatening, functional alternatives.

A psychologist suggested that a definition of greens as human beings wait "until we are absolutely certain about relative aggression levels."

Bradley Duncan responded that after living among greens for ten months he felt very comfrotable in concluding that greens were neither more nor less aggressive than were other Americans.

Daniel Adamson, throughout the long discussions, threatened. Ann Sullivan pleaded for understanding. And Gabriel reiterated his formal argument.

At 7:12 P.M., November 20, 2027, by a ten-vote margin, the conference passed a resolution. "The term 'human beings'," the final document stated, "shall be understood to include both those Homo sapiens who do and those who do not possess chlorophyll within their epidermal tissue."

Duncan and Batterson supported the resolution. Louise had abstained. "We have no more evidence than we did six months ago," she explained to Connie. "This is not a vote by scientists but by people invested with ideological values."

"Aren't we all?" Brad retorted.

Episode 17

Gabe nudged Ann Sullivan toward a sundries counter in the main terminal of the Phoenix airport. "Let's take a look at how the <u>Phoenix Herald</u> is reporting the conference vote yesterday," Gabriel said, plunking down a ten-dollar bill on the counter.

"I'm so tired," Ann smiled apologetically, "I don't even think I care."

Gabe gazed at his companion, then returned his attention to the counter clerk. "And give me a jar of those protein capsules," he said.

Gabriel pocketed his change, then handed the vial of tiny pills to Ann.

"What's this for?" she asked.

"Protein," Gabe said, matter-of-factly. "Take one. I found I needed them once in a while in Chicago. I took them all through the trial. You won't feel so tired."

"Thank you," Ann said simply. "Thank you." She put the vial of pills into her shoulder bag.

Daniel approached. "Where have you two been?" he demanded. "I've got the luggage. Alexander's here to take us home. Secret Service will escort us to the gates."

Daniel led Sullivan and Knapp to the waiting limousine.

"You three are heroes at home," Alexander announced, turning his vehicle to exit the airport. "We've got a big welcome planned. The band's been practicing all night long."

Gabriel sat quietly, remembering the time he had returned only to be attacked by Larry Jones's thugs. "Things change," he said finally.

"They're already talking about hiring outsiders at S.T.I. someday. The only thing that holds back expansion is our small labor force."

"Who's talking about that?" snapped Daniel.

"Mostly Jacob. He thinks it would be a good idea. Now that some of the greatest scientists in the world have defined us as human, he says, maybe outsiders will begin to stop threatening us."

The limousine wound its way up an entrance ramp to a divided highway. Inconspicuously Ann Sullivan placed a protein capsule upon her tongue and, working her cheeks to salivate, swallowed the energy source without water.

"The Elders won't be at the gates to meet us," Alexander informed

Key concepts:
Technology
Urbanism

---

his passengers later. "Ruth is in the hospital. The physicians say it could be serious."

"How serious?" asked Ann, surprised.

"Pretty serious," Alexander responded in his typical cursory manner.

"How is Michael taking it?" Gabriel inquired.

"Not well. He's doing almost nothing. Just sits in the parlor. Doesn't seem to care about much of anything now." Alexander paused. "But he does want to see you all today."

"When did Ruth become ill?" questioned Daniel.

"The morning after you left. I took her to the hospital that afternoon. She ordered that no one try to get a message to you. She wanted you to be able to concentrate on your work."

When the limousine passed the guard shelter and entered Adamsville, the group was met with band music and wild cheering. Greens of various shades spilled into the road both ahead and behind the advancing automobile. "Welcome, welcome" the throng chanted even above the blare of the band. "We're human!" many called.

Once in front of Elderhome Gabe, Ann, and Daniel were escorted up the front steps. But as the three moved to enter Elderhome, the spectacular celebration suddenly became a debacle. "Is Sullivan to come in too?" Gabriel overheard Daniel challenge Alexander.

Momentarily confused by Dan's question, Alexander hesitated. Before he opened his lips to respond, Gabriel had acted.

"Of course Ann's coming in with us," Knapp shouted while Adamsville watched in apprehension.

"She's a milk-white," Dan breathed from between clenched teeth.

At that moment Jacob appeared. "Welcome back, Gabe," he said calmly, extending his hand in an attempt to appease his long-time friend. "It's really very good to have you all home safely."

"What's going on here?" Gabriel demanded, still angry.

"Nothing. It's nothing. Ann can go in. After all," Jacob looked toward Daniel, "she's a hero."

Gabriel stared defiantly at Jacob. "That's not good enough," he shouted for all to hear. The crowd was silent with anticipation. "That's just not good enough anymore! Ann Sullivan goes in because she's green, because she lives here in Adamsville, because she's a good citizen of this community—or neither of us go in. She doesn't enter Elderhome as an exception to any rule about dull greens and their spiritual or genetic deficiencies. She enters as a valleyite—healthy and proud."

His words still resounding in the ears of his listeners, Gabriel stormed from Elderhome's front steps. Ann Sullivan, along with other dull greens, followed. That afternoon Gabe moved his belongings to an apartment in the valley.

Once the dissenters had departed, the crowd stood dumbfounded. The band director motioned quickly and again music played. Jacob led the throng across the street to the park where he urged they rest and take a quiet light-break "in thankful meditation for our victory."

Meanwhile Michael-the-Elder remained inside his home, wondering what was to become of Adamsville—and of his sister, Ruth. Daniel slumped into Sunlight Liquidhouse and ordered a glass of water. He would sit there brooding throughout the afternoon.

Three days later Ruth-the-Elder died. The morning of her burial Michael sent for Jacob. He directed that Larry Jones's shares of S.T.I. stock—since he had died intestate—be divided among Gabriel, Daniel, and Ann Sullivan in recognition for their accomplishments at the third conference. Then he signed his own and his sister's stock to Jacob. And he informed the younger man that, beginning the next day, it was to be Jacob who would govern Adamsville.

On November 29, 2027, in an elaborate ceremony Jacob was officially named "Successor Elder." During his speech which followed, he announced that S.T.I. would begin to plan for expansion. There would be diversification, including funding for genetic research on human mutations. Results from this kind of research would someday allow descendants of mutants to establish by computer the amounts of protein intake they individually required. "Technological knowledge such as this," Jacob promised, "can one day work to decrease both greens' and ungreens' fear of assimilation."

Gabriel Knapp was not to remain in Adamsville, however, to watch these planned technological changes become reality. "I think we should move down to Phoenix," he said one day in December to Ann Sullivan.

"Move?" she repeated.

"Yes. The whole lot of us. There are no services here for us. We have to go several miles to buy protein. We still stand huddled in frightened little groups near the edges of the crowd when anyone speaks from the platform. Jacob, in his fear of disturbing the remaining radical militarists, has not officially changed any of the rules that discriminate against us."

"Move?" Ann said again.

"Here you work as a guard," Gabriel pursued, "And I put in routine hours at S.T.I. In Phoenix we could at least try to find work we like."

He paused, trying to read the woman's thoughts.

"You wouldn't have to sneak your protein capsules for fear of ridicule in Phoenix," he said. "The whole group of us from the valley could go. We could find ourselves an area of the city we like and live there together."

"I have to think about it," Ann said.

The thinking and planning lasted several weeks. To fellow valleyites Gabriel argued that in Phoenix dull greens would spend most of their time in their own neighborhood, just as was true in Adamsville. But in the city valleyites would be virtually unrecognizable outside their own neighborhood. It was true that when ungreens recognized them as mutants, his people could expect to suffer from discrimination. But for the most part, valleyites would go unnoticed. "How many of you will go?" Jacob inquired of Gabriel during an official conference at Elderhome.

"Twenty-five. Maybe thirty," Gabe said.

"We need those people at S.T.I.," insisted Jacob.

"We need a larger place," Gabriel answered.

Episode 18

"Dry-roasted soybeans!" Ann Sullivan giggled, lifting a jar from the shipping crate she was unpacking and placing it on a shelf above her head.

"Chocolate-covered raisins?" Gabriel laughed, setting the vacuum-packed container on another shelf opposite Ann. "You've got to be kidding!"

It was evening, March 19, 2028. Four months earlier the two had returned victorious from the third conference on human mutations.

"You know what I miss?" Gabe said, suddenly melancholy. "I miss spring in Chicago."

"You're not happy here in Phoenix?" Ann questioned.

During the previous January Gabriel and twenty-seven other valleyites had moved into a modest neighborhood on the northeast edge of Phoenix. With dividends drawn from Gabriel's and Ann Sullivan's S.T.I. stock, the group had purchased three small homes, a rooming house, and a vacant storefront in which Ann planned to open a delicatessen. Gabriel lived in the rooming house while Sullivan shared one of the homes with several other valleyites, among them her former roommates.

"It's Lake Michigan, I guess," Gabe said now, more to himself than to his companion. "I miss the way the wind comes in over the lake."

"Maybe you can go back someday," Ann cheered. Then she paused; when she spoke again her voice was lower. "Are you glad you came to Phoenix, Gabriel?"

Gabe smiled. "I think we will make ourselves a comfortable neighborhood here," he said. "I just wish the desert had one of the Great Lakes, that's all."

"And I just wish this place were ready to open," Ann played. "I'd invite everyone down after the maturing ceremony for a refreshment-filled weekend."

Gabe laughed. "Can't you just see Dan Adamson in here? 'How about some salted peanuts, Dan? Care for an apple?' 'Oh, thank you, no,' he'd say. 'Actually I'm too perfect to need to eat'."

It was the eve of Gabriel's maturation ceremony. "I have to go back for it," he had explained earlier to some other former valleyites. "Jonathan, my soft parent, would want it."

Ann Sullivan set the last jar of roasted soybeans in place and bent

Key concepts:
Mass communication
Public opinion
Social change
Social construction of reality

---

to take the empty shipping container outside. Near the doorway she stopped, turning back toward Gabriel. "Did you see the paper today?" she asked.

"No. Why?"

"The *Phoenix Herald* did a front-page feature on the maturing ceremony tomorrow. I haven't had a chance to read it closely. Take a look."

Gabe recovered a newspaper that lay on the floor amid an assortment of partially unpacked boxes. The *Phoenix Herald* had, since its first spectacular story on the mutants, remained interested in Adamsville, and now the prospect of an article on the maturation ceremony intrigued Gabe.

He read for several seconds, noting the general accuracy of presentation. It was evident that the journalist responsible for the story had done some homework.

When he had completed what was carried of the story on the front page, he moved to open the paper to page 4 where the piece continued.

Suddenly his attention was grabbed by a headline positioned in the lower right-hand corner of the front page. Ann must have missed this, he thought, his heart beginning to pound.

"Mother of Kidnapped Chicago Infant Commits Suicide," the headline clamored. Gabriel read the story:

"Chicago—Sarah Welsh, mother of the infant boy kidnapped from Lake Hospital June 28, 2026, has hanged herself at a local mental hospital here. She was found in her room shortly before 5 A. M., authorities said . . .

"It was widely circulated at the time of the kidnapping that the infant was stolen by green mutants whose religion makes virtue of such practice . . .

"Gabriel Knapp, once an executive with Chicago National Insurance and, according to reputable sources, a green mutant, was tried and acquitted of the kidnapping. According to reports he now resides in Phoenix."

Ann returned to the room. "Is it *that* biased?" she asked, noting the expression on Gabriel's face.

"I've got to go," he said, rising to leave and handing the newspaper to Ann. "I'll see you in the morning."

Three cars filled with former valleyites arrived at Adamsville the next forenoon. "It doesn't look like they've had any recent border trouble," Ann remarked, noting the relaxed posture of the young green in the guard shelter.

"And no more state police," Gabe said, recalling the first time he had heard the derogatory term "greenface."

That day at noon Gabriel donned a velvet ceremonial cloak and, with five others from the community, ascended the sacred platform. He looked out into a sea of green faces. Behind him on the platform sat Michael, weak with age.

When he had removed his green cape, Jacob began the politico-spiritual litany. "We are the future people of the earth," he chanted. "We are the culmination of God's evolutionary plan."

That afternoon inside the Great Hall Gabriel grew pensive. Incidents from recent years, in no apparent order, crowded into his brain. He recalled lying upon the earth, sand grinding its way into his face and eyes. He recalled Monica and the July Fourth picnic he once shared with her. He remembered the day he received the medical report; he pictured his office at Chicago National. He recalled the rescue. The trial. He remembered peering curiously into a tiny baby's eyes while he sat holding him on an airplane. He recalled vomiting into a dirty lavatory sink the day he heard that the child was dead.

He thought of the physical beauty of Rebecca Lockwood—and of Larry Jones. He recalled Jonathan Knapp, his soft parent. He thought of his long, academic discussions with Connie Batterson. And of his tormenting confession to Monica. And he thought of a woman whom he had never met: Sarah Welsh.

Jacob approached. "Congratulations, Gabe," he said, embracing his friend. "How long can you stay? I have plenty of room, you know."

"I think we'll be getting on back tonight," Gabe said. "Several of us have to work tomorrow."

Jacob stood a minute, not sure of what to say. "Well," he forced a grin, disappointed to see his friend leave so soon, "maybe someday I'll get down to Phoenix. Think it's safe for bright greens like me yet?"

"Not yet. Someday maybe," Gabe said.

Jacob drew in a breath, changing the subject. "Michael would like to visit with you before you go."

When Gabriel entered Elderhome an hour later, he was ushered by Alexander to Michael's private bedroom. The old man lay quietly upon his bed, bathed in a sea of fluorescent light.

"Elder?" Gabriel spoke softly. "Gabriel," Michael murmured. "I am about to die."

Gabe sat down on a chair beside Michael's bed, saying nothing.

"I'm glad you matured," Michael said.

"Yes," Gabriel whispered.

"Do you enjoy living in Phoenix?"

"It is not paradise," Gabriel smiled. "But it is a place for us."

Michael struggled with his words. "Tell me, are you glad that you were raised here in Adamsville?"

Gabe stared. "I had never thought about it that way," he said. "I am a green; it was necessary that I be raised here."

"You are thankful then that you were rescued?"

"Of course, Elder."

"I'm glad," Michael said. "I'm very glad."

The two sat for a long time. "Can I get you anything?" Gabe offered.

"Our people are beginning to question now," Michael said, peering into the light above him. "Some outsiders work at S. T. I. now. They raise questions. Adamsvillers have begun to wonder."

"Wonder about rescuing?" Gabriel asked.

Michael nodded.

Gabriel took Michael's thin, green hand. "I am glad that I was rescued," he reaffirmed. "It was necessary."

It was to be the last conversation Gabriel would have with Michael-the-Elder.

A few minutes before midnight the party arrived back in Phoenix. As Gabe walked alone to his rooming house, Ann Sullivan came up behind him, taking his sleeve. "Can we talk a minute?" she asked.

"Sure," he said, turning in the darkness, "what is it?"

"No one mentioned Larry Jones today. Did you notice?"

Gabe shuffled. "To keep talking about him would only stir up old animosities," Gabe suggested. "It's better this way."

"Gabriel," Ann said, "why did you never attempt to find out who shot him?"

"There would have been no point to it," he said. "After the assassination Jacob and I discussed it and he felt the same way. To go through a long investigation would only have ripped apart a community that was already dangerously divided."

"I killed him," Ann confessed suddenly.

Gabriel stepped back. "Why are you telling me this now?"

"I don't know," she said. "It haunts me." .

"I understand that," Gabe responded, his mind turning again to Sarah Welsh. "I have been responsible for death also."

Episode 19

It was in late June of the year 2032 that Monica appeared at Gabriel's door. She arrived with Louise Roanoke.

Gabriel had just returned from his office at Southwest Insurance and changed his clothes when he heard the bell. Flicking off the exposed fluorescent tubing in his bedroom he walked, curious, through a large, glass-roofed garden room to open his front door.

"Gabe?"

He recognized the voice even before he looked into her face.

"It's been over four years!" he heard himself exclaiming seconds later.

"Louise and I are on our way back to Chicago from Mexico City," Monica was explaining. "We're between planes. We thought we'd stop."

"Come in," he managed.

When his guests were seated he asked whether they would like something.

"Maybe some wine," Monica said.

"Yes, thank you, Gabriel," Louise added, "wine would be good."

Gabriel went to a wet bar, removed the cork from a bottle of burgundy, and carried it and three glasses into the garden room. Returning to the bar, he fixed a plate of soybean chips and assorted cheeses.

"Snacks?" Monica asked upon seeing the food. "Gabriel Knapp, you've changed!"

"Not as much as you might think," he responded. "But I keep a few things around now. I like a little cheese every so often. Remember Ann Sullivan? Or perhaps you didn't meet her. *You* met her though, Dr. Roanoke"—he turned to face the older woman, already aware that he had begun to ramble nervously—"well, Ann Sullivan opened a little deli a few blocks from here about four years ago now. I helped her stock the shelves. Handling all that silly stuff made me curious, I guess." Gabriel stopped abruptly. "What are you doing now, Monica?"

"I'm still with the firm," she said. "Although I'm thinking about leaving soon. I'd like to take off on my own. Open a little office somewhere in a low-rent neighborhood and answer my own phone. That sort of thing."

"Are you still with Civil Liberty for All?"

"Oh, yes," she said, "I've tried several cases for them. Nothing as spectacular as yours though."

112

Key concept:
Sociology as a profession

Gabriel took a swallow of wine. "Will you stay in Chicago?" he asked.

"Probably," she said. "We like Chicago."

"We?"

She gazed at him. "I married two years ago," she said.

He didn't reply.

"We have a little girl."

"Oh," he answered, "wonderful." His voice trailed off. He remembered that he and Monica used to talk about that sometimes.

"Tell me, Gabriel," Louise said, "how is Daniel Adamson, the other delegate who came with you to the conference?"

"Fine," Gabe said. "Just fine. He's still up in Adamsville, of course. He matured last year. His skin is brilliant. He publishes a newspaper in the colony now. Quite a radical, very separatist paper, from what I've seen. But generally the community is more liberal now. Daniel speaks to a minority."

"And Ann Sullivan owns a delicatessen here, you say?" Louise pursued, academically curious.

"Yes. She's running for the Arizona State Legislature. She worked very hard to get the state's ban on intermarriage declared unconstitutional last year."

"Whatever happened to the federal bill that would have denied greens the right to vote in federal elections?" Louise asked Monica.

"It was permanently tabled shortly after the third conference," Monica replied. She turned toward Gabe. "I read a few years ago in the papers that you matured," she said.

"Yes," Gabe answered.

"Do you go back to Adamsville often?" Monica asked, placing a slice of cheese on a soybean chip.

"Every few months." He paused. "There are unpleasant memories there, but then there are many good ones too." "Well, tell me," he shifted, "how is Bradley Duncan?"

"He's down in Brazil now," Louise said, "doing a study on possible ways to improve the health of native tribes."

"And drinking Brazilian beer," Monica added with a laugh.

"I went to the university library here and looked up his journal article on word meanings in Adamsville," Gabriel said. "I enjoyed it."

113

"What he's doing now may prove even more useful to a greater number of people," Louise smiled.

"And where is Dr. Batterson?" Gabe asked.

"She and her husband are in Africa," Louise answered, "helping to organize the labor movement there. The study she was doing on discrimination toward greens was published in *Transaction* last year."

"Some sociologists from the University of Arizona," Gabriel offered, sipping his wine, "are doing research on problems our children may face when they begin to attend school here in Phoenix."

"Your community here is growing then," Monica concluded.

"Yes," Gabe nodded. "We have done well here. We have encountered some discrimination, of course, but we expected that. We have been very lucky that even in spite of prejudice many of us have found satisfying jobs—often in the areas for which we were educated and trained while posing." He shifted, conscious that he had gone on too long. "And, Louise, what are you doing now?"

"I'll be teaching at the University of Mexico City this fall. That's why I spent the last two weeks there. I wanted to check into living space, things like that. Monica came along for a vacation." Dr. Roanoke drank from her glass of burgundy.

"Tell me more about Adamsville," Monica requested. "It must be quite different now in some ways."

"Well," Gabe began, "pure greens continue to live within the boundaries. The fence is still up, and guards are still posted. But for the most part there is no trouble near the borders, and the guards are more a tradition than a necessity. A friend of mine from childhood, Jacob, is Elder. He moved into Elderhome after Michael's death.

"Many outsiders work at S.T.I. now. Their presence has influenced some changes. Some residents are beginning to talk about electing a mayor by secret ballot, as outsiders do, rather than accepting Jacob as Michael's chosen successor."

"Has Adamsville's religion changed?" Louise asked.

"Some, yes," Gabe said. "Light-break, for example, is now considered more a necessity to a mutant's good health than a religious exercise. Few would consider it prayer. But there remain those orthodox greens—many who once supported Larry Jones—who insist that the truths set down by Adam must never change. This is one reason I persuaded many from the valley to come to Phoenix. In Adamsville many continued to think of us as spiritually degenerate. And even the liberals considered us sick, genetically deficient."

"And are you happy here now?" asked Monica.

"Yes," Gabriel affirmed. "I'm comfortable here."

"Do you live here alone?"

"No," Gabe answered. "Three others whom neither of you know

and I entered a five-year friendship contract last summer. We designed and built this home last fall shortly after one of us was admitted to practice medicine on the staff at Central Hospital—and after I was promoted at Southwest Insurance."

"You're back in the insurance business then," Monica smiled.

"Yes," Gabe nodded. "We're developing standards of coverage for both pure and partial mutants. There's no doubt in my mind that we'll be offering health coverage to greens within five years."

Louise glanced at her watch. "I'm sorry this visit was so brief," she apologized, standing up. "But I'm afraid it's time we were getting back to the airport."

"I'll take you," Gabriel offered.

"No," Monica said. "It's already been arranged. A taxi is coming for us." She paused, aware of Gabe's—and her own—disappointment. "We couldn't be sure whether we'd find you—or whether you'd be free—"

"I understand," Gabe interrupted her explanation.

The cab had returned and was parked near the curb. Louise shook Gabriel's hand. "I very much enjoyed seeing you again," she said. "Thank you for the wine and food." Then she left the home and walked toward the waiting taxi.

"Listen," Gabe said to Monica, "keep in touch."

"You too," she said, turning to leave.